T0196383

Yoshi's Paintbrush

LESSONS IN NONCONFORMITY

Rune Marie Nielsen

AuthorHouse™
1663 Liberty Drive
Bloomington, IN 47403
www.authorhouse.com
Phone: 1-800-839-8640

Published by AuthorHouse 05/24/2013

ISBN: 978-1-4817-5653-2 (sc)
ISBN: 978-1-4817-5652-5 (e)

Library of Congress Control Number: 2013909516

This book is printed on acid-free paper.

Dedicated to my kindergarten teacher Mrs. Fosson, who believed in my storytelling ability before I could read or write. Special thanks to my sister Lisa Murray, without whom this book would not have found the courage to publish itself.

I wrote this novel when I was fifteen years old and recently at age twenty-three I edited it for publication. Many of the illustrations in this book combine images from sketches I drew at age fifteen and artwork I have completed this year.

Pronunciation Guide:

Yoshi (yo-shee)
Joshi (yo-shee)
Ioshi (yo-shee)
Jaaski (yo-shee)

For more stories and comics, go to www.jaaski.com.

Table of Contents

1. No takeout, no chopsticks 1
2. The chapter after chapter one; Yoshi to Joshi 10
3. Between the earth and soul 24
4. The chapter that wouldn't end 30
5. In the Realm of the Toilet 42
6. Be sure to flush before you leave 53
7. Who reads chapter titles, anyway? 65
8. Sincerely but not sincere 77
9. Find a problem for the solution 89
10. Mir ist Schwindlig (Me is dizzy) 102
11. A severe case of mental constipation 116
12. Welcome to knighthood, Sir Joshi 129
13. A dragon named Snarg 140
14. Joshi in Wonderland 151
15. Deleted Memory 166
16. Insert title here 179
17. Watch out, Mr. Fuzzyhead 192
18. I'm Not Krazy 205
19. The chapter that never happened and never will ... 216
20. Zippy's back!!! 222

Chapter 1

No takeout, no chopsticks

Noodles. Fresh, slippery, warm magic-in-your-mouth noodles. The kind that makes your mind utter a secret *Yay!* while everyone else stares at their food. Or, if you are Yoshi this is what you do. Little did Yoshi know that an innocent bowl of noodles had absolutely nothing to do with the misfortunes that lay ahead. The steam from the microwaved udon bowl rose like smoke from a volcano, but Yoshi failed to notice this ominous symbolism. Instead she contented herself with blowing on the steam as if it were full of bubbles to be popped.

"Ah, thank you, Hitoshi," said Yoshi with an air of triumph upon receiving her hard-earned (yet free) udon from the office errand boy. Hitoshi nodded and went about his merry way putting udon bowls on the desks of Yoshi's coworkers, many of which did not even look up to acknowledge the blissful food in front of them.

There she was, Yoshi Tokio, reclining in a wheeled chair—a blue wheeled chair—staring out the window—a blue window—of the Junior Graphics Department in the headquarters—a blue headquarters—of *Blue Ninja* Magazine. She was proud to be a Japanese girl, also part Chinese and part Korean, twelve years old with long black hair and thick bangs, thicker and flatter than the hair anywhere else on her scalp. Covering those bangs, flattening the already flat hair, was a baseball cap—a blue baseball cap—that said something in Japanese on it. Yoshi opened the zipper to her canvas art bag—I shall now stop pointing out the colors of objects—and took out her personal sketchbook—which unfortunately was not blue, but gray (sorry I lied).

Yoshi reached into her paintbrush bag with a smile. This time she would use a new paintbrush, 'new' in the sense that she had never used it before. What had yesterday shown cracks and exposed wood was now quite usable. After she rescued the broken paintbrush out of a trash can she lovingly cemented together its splintered wood with craft glue and rolled it in gloss medium to keep the surface smooth. And thus it took its place among the other inconspicuous paintbrushes in her bag.

Yoshi swirled the newly refurbished paintbrush in some water and got to work. On a noodle-ly day such as this, one couldn't help but think of mischief.

"All I want is . . . a dog!" And she began to paint a dog, as was the common subject in all of her artwork. No better way to celebrate eating noodles than to think of something else you want. A dash of ink and a speck of color, and then . . . . Well, there was just another dog on the paper.

"My dog would be much cooler than normal. It would be . . . like me! Only different." And at that moment a brand new idea entered her head. *Brand* new ideas are very hard to come by. Most ideas are just *new*. It started with only one word to hear.

"Zippy!" And little did she know that Zippy was here to stay. "I'll call it a space—dog, a dog from another universe. She'll be blue with big ears and purple spots. She'll speak to me in a robotic voice, but will not be a machine. She will be intelligent and also fun to be around. My dog's name will be Zippedity Zhong, in short, Zippy."

Zippy had landed.

"Hello, I am Zippy," said a robotic voice. Yoshi looked down and saw a multicolored puppy sitting at her feet wagging its tail. Yoshi blinked five times before realizing that she had the wonderful misfortune of bringing to life a creature on paper.

"Zippy, you must hide! If someone sees . . ." Where to put the dog? Under her desk?

"Sees what? Sees that you have found the un-forbidden paintbrush of personalities?" said Zippy.

Squeak . . . Yoshi heard the slow squeal of a rolling chair scooting out from someone's desk.

"Hide in my mind and I shall use this paintbrush to call you out." Yoshi hardly knew what she was saying. Zippy's words almost made more sense to her.

"Agreed, Yoshi-san. Let the kaos begin."

Zippy knew all too well that *kaos* is the ultra-hyper form of *chaos.* All Yoshi knew was that she was about to experience it for herself.

The following weeks Yoshi only needed to hold the newly-old paintbrush and call out to Zippy with her thoughts in order to summon Zippy from her mind. Doing so brought the dog into the tangible world around her, often her room, a rather ordinary but tiny hideout with four plaster walls, carpet floor, a bed, desk, and file cabinet. When someone dared attempt to intrude on Yoshi's private space with a disgruntled knock on the door, she only had to call Zippy back into her mind with a brief thought.

Zippy was full of strange advice (and also full of the noodles Yoshi fed to her).

"The world isn't as blue as the Abyss," said Zippy.

"What is the Abyss?" asked Joshi.

"It is your mind and how you view it."

But all too soon Zippy began to jump out of Yoshi's mind on her own without Yoshi's approval. Yoshi liked hearing Zippy talk with her uniquely robotic voice, but once Zippy began staying in Yoshi's bedroom on her own Yoshi also had the pleasure of cleaning up after Zippy's sock fights and Zippy's sharpening of all pencils on both ends (and the attempted sharpening of pens). Zippy was a messy roommate, but she was a dog, after all. Along with all of this disarray, Joshi discovered a mysterious decrease in her supply of toilet paper. Yoshi was particularly alert about it because her major chore at home was to unclog clogged toilets. Sometimes while she was plunging a toilet Zippy would sit on the toilet tank and talk to her. The two of them discussed politics, science, history, subatomic particles, and psychology, among other topics favorable to an alien dog.

After school and on weekends Yoshi had fun playing the board game go with an opponent for once, (even if it her opponent was just a step above an imaginary friend) as well as throwing darts with Zippy. She wished she wasn't so lonely at school, however (and she did feel bad that Zippy won every single time they played darts). School was a void without friends. Or excessive amounts of blue objects. Or noodles. She wanted a best friend as much as she'd ever wanted a pet dog, a friend who could go places with her and agree that Biology was hard (for nothing seemed too difficult for Zippy).

One particular evening Yoshi made the mistake of going to bed thinking about this complex topic.

The next morning Yoshi woke up not feeling like herself. But, being herself, she rolled out of bed like she did every morning. Except this time she fell on the floor. She could never have fallen on the floor before because her Japanese bed was on the floor. She rubbed a sore spot on her head and looked at the bed. This bed was two feet off the ground—two feet too much. The blanket's design was similar to the dragon print of her Japanese bed, except that this comforter had straight-backed Norse dragons instead of the wavy scales of zodiac dragons.

In a panic she looked around the room at other things, a wooden desk pushed against the wall with a window above it, a closet, and a file cabinet. A file cabinet just like the one she had in the room she went to sleep in, in *her* room. Or did she have a file cabinet? Yes, she did, but . . . right now was a very bad time for forgetting normal things. How could her memory be wrong?

Yoshi ran to the file cabinet in the corner of the room and looked for anything that was the same as before, any papers she recognized. When she pulled open the first metal drawer the only item she spotted was a pair of shiny snow boots made of bright aqua green rubber. On the shoe laces was a label that said "Yoshi boots." She pulled open the second drawer of the file cabinet. *Clang, clang clang* creaked the drawer's wheels against the sides.

In a flash of purple sparks Zippy jumped out of the drawer and into Yoshi's mind. Before Yoshi knew it, she was standing in front of a mirror, still in her pajamas. Beside her stood a girl that looked exactly like her but with a devious smirk on her face.

Yoshi couldn't imagine herself making such an expression, mouth stretched wide with one end slyly curving upward, an eyebrow slanted down towards the curve of the lips, and most of all, deep, penetrating eyeballs that seemed to stare through everything.

"I will duplicate another body for you to have." said Zippy's voice in the identical smirking girl standing next to Yoshi.

"But I want to be myself!" Yoshi said.

"You will be," said Zippy still speaking robotically, "Only different."

Zippy spun Yoshi around and had her look in the mirror again. Zippy looked like the same clone of herself, but Yoshi had changed.

"This girl is American, and I think she's just as pretty as you! I've made you look just like her, only not."

Not quite understanding Zippy's explanation, Yoshi replied, "But what if I don't want to be pretty?" To look beautiful was certainly a dumb reason to change one's appearance, but it turned out that was indeed not Zippy's reason.

Yoshi remained in the body of the American girl, but Zippy's appearance was morphing. Zippy assimilated her alien features she had before as a dog into the body she now inhabited, still looking like the Japanese Yoshi, except with purple eyes, much larger alienish ears, and two very noticeable snail eyes on antennae poking out of the top of her head.

With one goodbye, Zippy began to fade away. "I'll be in Tokyo" she said. Only this time her voice was not robotic, but deep and gruff (and a tad bit scary); unrealistic, but humanish.

Yoshi looked back in the mirror. She realized she was in a bathroom with a very large painting of a blue sailboat on the moon hanging above the toilet. Then she noticed what she looked like. Her hair was short and strawberry blonde with blue edges. Her eyes were still dark brown and a little bit red and her skin was now very, very pale.

Unsure of what to do next, Yoshi ran out to the hallway where she spotted another file cabinet, this one with two drawers. She pulled open the first drawer. There was nothing in it except for a small piece of folded paper. Yoshi unfolded it and read in English "No takeout, no chopsticks—policy of Zippedity Zhong, Bad Ideas, Inc." What had appeared to be an ad or a fortune cookie riddle might be both an advertisement slogan and a trick of wits. Yoshi kicked the drawer shut and reached for the one remaining drawer in the file cabinet she hadn't touched.

"Nuh-uh-uh!" echoed a strangely familiar voice.

"You, still in my head!!!" Yoshi sputtered.

"Well, not exactly," said Zippy, "You see, this is a back-up file of me. I thought I'd duplicate myself so I'd be here for you—even while I'm taking your place over yonder."

". . ." Joshi replied, not the happiest of confused people at the moment, although her curiosity was thrilled at the suspense of the situation. If curiosity killed cats, could it kill dogs, too? This could get dangerous.

"You can't open the second drawer yet because you haven't heard the explanation of the first. As my motto states, you can't get chopsticks without the effort of showing up for takeout. You can't find what you want until you make effort to search for it. Dreaming about something brings delight, but not success. You have to do instead of just think. Cooperate with yourself, that's what I say, Sport."

After a pause the voice of Zippy ended the greeting. "Takeout, yeah, like I said . . . I'm hungry for takeout." and her ghostly presence was gone.

Yoshi looked down at the unopened drawer in the filing cabinet. Where was she? What was Zippy? What were the rules of this arrangement? To find the answers, she knew there was only one thing to do . . .

CHAPTER 2

The chapter after chapter one: Yoshi to Joshi

Very cautiously at a snail's pace Yoshi pulled open the second drawer of the mysterious file cabinet. Inside it held neat stacks of papers orderly organized in a very arranged fashion. In other words, it looked like an ordinary file cabinet found in any office, anywhere. She sighed. Aware of Zippy's nontraditional ways of transmitting information, she had been expecting musical fireworks to pop in her face or any other special effect to happen, like a shower of confetti made from noodles.

Without a second thought Yoshi pulled out the manila folder at the very front. She opened the cover and . . . *BOOM*! All of the other folders and papers that had been neatly situated in the small compartment of the cabinet had evaporated into small twinkling snails floating in midair.

For the second time in the last thirty seconds, Yoshi was surprised.

"Read, read!" the snails squeaked in high-pitched voices like cutesy door bell chimes. Yoshi had to admit to herself that clearly Zippy's creativity out-smarted her own.

The snails were far from finished with their speech, however. "The more you know, the more you can be! Be, be! Be who you are! If there's any advice we can give you, it's this: Nothing stinks as much as caviar!" With that, the snails took off at top speed (averaging 30 centimeters per hour) gliding through the air and out the window to who knows where. Yoshi had never smelled caviar, much less been in the same room as caviar, so she figured she had nothing to fear.

She returned her attention to the documents in her hand and carefully examined the paper-clipped packets with intrigue. A second glance at the cover of the folder revealed a label on the tab that said "Joshi," typed in blue with a paw print dotting the 'i.' She could have sworn no such text was present on the folder tab before now.

"*GJJawsh-ee*? . . . No, perhaps *GJo-shee* . . ." An even closer look revealed paint stains and fingerprints along the cover and inside pages, the first of which seemed to be a biography about someone with a photograph stapled to it.

Name:	Joshi
Status:	loner, tomboy
Archetype:	anti-hero, shadow

Nationality:	half Skandinavian, half? (wants to be an elf, claims to have an invisible tail)
Bloodtype:	O negative (because the glass is half empty)
Eyes:	dark
Hair:	short and yellow (NOT blonde), with bangs, sometimes blue (depends on mood)
Stature:	gaunt
Kringle:	cold, with hot chocolate
Diet:	carnivorous

In addition Yoshi found a long list of "Character Speech Patterns" tucked behind the biography. Beneath the entire stack of papers she found her lucky baseball cap, still rounded in form, oddly unaffected by the weight of the paper and the slim shape of the folder. The word above the bill was no longer in Japanese, for it now said "Sport." Yoshi put it on immediately in hopes of feeling normal again. Also in the folder was her favorite magazine, only now with a different title. "Skrive" it read across the top. She picked up the magazine and flipped through it, realizing that her work that was in last month's issue of *Blue Ninja* had been translated into a different language.

As she turned the last page a folded piece of cardstock paper floated to the ground. It was a city map, amazingly detailed to show every single object and piece of furniture between her and the next two blocks. A yellow smiley face was drawn in crayon around the words "file cabinet, where you are now." Yoshi traced her finger along a yellow dotted line from the file cabinet to a building located down the street where it was written, "Destination: Come here with your folder and its contents! Please!"

Feeling she had no choice, Joshi changed into some clothes she found in the closet pulled on her Yoshi boots and walked out with her folder under her arm. Maybe she'd find some answers and a plane ticket home (because wherever this was it definitely wasn't Japan). After all, she was wearing her lucky cap (her only hat) and lucky boots (her only shoes). What she wouldn't have guessed was that she was going to get a lot more answers than she bargained for.

Yoshi looked up. The sign on the building read "Character Data Center." A fire hydrant with dog poop next to it stood to the side of the building, as shown on the map. She walked in, stepping over a wad of squishy gum on the entrance mat, as had also been shown on the map.

A young clerk no older than thirteen sat behind a counter nearest the door gnawing on a gum wrapper. Above him was a sign that said in all caps, bold letters "**CONFUSEMENT CASES**." Yoshi's gut feeling told her this was the place she needed to go. *Be polite and get out of here*, she told herself.

"Excuse me, I've been told to come here due to a recent change in character by way of paper data."

"Yapf, this is where they send you when that happenses. Present paperwork evidence, miss."

Yoshi placed the folder on the counter. The clerk grabbed a scan-like machine mounted to the wall behind the counter and ran a neon light over the folder. The light blinked and buzzed every couple seconds. Was he searching for theft like the scanners at supermarket exits? Then the scanner started to make louder noises, beepity noises, ones that would bounce off sound waves at random tempos and pitches—an odd song of humming sound effects out of tune.

Is it supposed to do that? Yoshi wondered to herself.

"This maw-sheen counts how many words there air' written all over these-es pages. The more beeps, the more words-es. The more words-es, the longer your confusement. Makes things mores ek-sitting, yapf?" Just his way of speaking seemed enough to confuse anyone unfamiliar with it.

At that moment the neon scanner stopped beeping and flashed a number on a small screen on its handle:—599,950. Yoshi didn't think there could possibly be 599,950 words on three pages. She was about to tell the young clerk the machine must be broken, but then a phone below the counter rang.

"Yapf? Oh, yapf, client nummer thirty-five iss here. Yapf, will do. Thanks you, bye-eeee."

He put down the phone and spat the gum wrapper out of his mouth into a trashcan. "*Negative* 599, 950. So many words missing, so great a way to finds them. Life is full of searchings for lost things, yapf?"

Yoshi nodded, beginning to get a slight idea of what might be going on, though she wouldn't be able to explain what.

"I em goings to ask you some questions, and you musts provide meee with answers to each one, miss."

Yoshi took a deep breath and nodded sternly, like a student ready to take a final exam.

"What is your name? Write it down here." He put down a pen and a blank nametag on the counter. Text written on the pen said "Do not eat this pen. It has ink in it. It would occur you a bad problem."

Yoshi didn't know why anyone would assume a pen had no ink left in it and want to eat it. She also did not think there was such a thing as a problem that was not bad, that's why problems were troublesome, like math problems. But Yoshi was only in her twelfth year of breathing, eating, and sleeping, and she was aware of her childishness. A kid like her was used to being confused about not knowing everything. Fortunately for Yoshi, she had not yet discovered that the feeling would only get worse when she reached adulthood.

Yoshi timidly picked up the pen and started to write, only to discover there was indeed no ink coming out of the pen.

"Umm, this pen doesn't seem to be working. I think it's out of ink."

The young clerk wrinkled his eyebrows. "People assume so much—assumings thingies are broken just because they don't work eks-actly the way they ek-spect them to. Did you tell it to write?"

Yoshi shook her head.

"Then just asks it."

"Okay . . ."

Yoshi whispered in her mind "Please work, ink. Please work, pen." And despite feeling stupid for doing such a bizarre thing, she was relieved that it actually worked. She wrote "Yoshi" on the nametag and showed it to the clerk.

"My name is Yo–"

"What's this? *Y-o-s-h-i*? I don't thinks I can pronounce that. It doesn't seems feasible. Ah, look at thats, the ink isn't sticking to the paper just yet." He pointed to the nametag where just as he'd said, the ink was sliding off the paper into air and dissolving. "Try it differentlys. Y'know, the better beginning of something makes way for a better end."

Yoshi didn't understand how her name could be wrong. How could *she* get the wrong answer for *her* name? She wanted to tell the clerk that his questions weren't 'feasible' (whatever he meant by that), but then Yoshi felt something poking her left foot. She squatted on the floor and reached into her left "Yoshi boot." Something long and hard was poking her near her heel. She grasped it and took out . . . a paintbrush? Yes, it was a paintbrush, and yes, it had been in her shoe. The paintbrush said something on it in undecipherable runic letters. She flipped it over, lucky to find a translation: "Ioshi / Joshi." But the letters didn't add up; there were more letters in the alphabetic translation, which produced two words, while the runic was obviously one. She showed the paintbrush to the young clerk.

"I see. Your name is *Joshi.*"

"That's what I told you!!! I also wrote it down!"

"No, what you had written down was *Yoshi.* This runic can be translated as either Joshi or Ioshi because in runic, 'J' and 'I' share the same letter. Guess you'll nevers really know if you're Joshi or Ioshi . . . unless . . . ah, neverminds. I think you are Joshi, but I could never be sure." *He* was unsure? Shouldn't he trust *her* to know her own name?

Yoshi wrote "Joshi" on the nametag and waited a good five seconds to see if the letters stuck. None fell off the nametag. She said, "I am Joshi."

The clerk pulled himself up onto the counter and stretched out his hand. Joshi shook it and statically shocked him the process.

"Kool name, Joshi. I am Jÿger." How was *kool* different from *cool*? But never mind that, Joshi told herself. There were much bigger puzzles to figure out.

"Now, what you musts do is put on your nametag. It doesn't haves to be visible, because-es only you and a few others will see it."

Yoshi didn't understand the purpose of a nametag if not everyone else could see it, but she complied, and stuck the name tag on the outer sole of her left Yoshi boot.

"Good choice. I keep my nametag close to my soul, too." Jÿger took off his shoe and showed Joshi his nametag, which was on the bottom of his sock. What did the *sole* of a shoe have to do with a *soul*? Maybe Joshi had more questions than Jÿger. He continued his interrogation.

"Next question. What color is your hair?"

Joshi wasn't sure why he had to get her to say what her hair color was if he could just see for himself.

After Joshi said nothing, Jÿger gave a suggestion for a possible answer. "Strawberry blonde? Yapf, a blondie you 'air." Jÿger held out a form and began to write "blonde" on one of the lines. "So, you're blon-"

"Skrumfidag! You are not to say I'm blonde! My hair is yellow, Jÿger. You are the blonde one!" And indeed he was, for his hair was much lighter than her own.

"Sorry, miss. Will do, yapf! . . ." And with a swish of placing his hand sideways on his forehead he saluted Joshi. "But, hej, you're already beginning to follow your speech patterns." Jÿger opened Joshi's folder and pointed to the word *Skrumfidag* on the list of speech patterns. There was even more for Joshi to figure out. Why did *hej* sound the same as *hey*?

"Okay, Joshi. There's only one more important question left." He leaned closer to her, a serious look in his eye. She didn't see how the other questions had been important, but she played along anyway.

"Can you answer this last question, Joshi? If you can't . . . it shall be . . . Well, it shall be very annoying for mee because I'll haves ek-stra paperwork to do." He laughed nervously and then returned to his serious look. "So, can you answers it, Joshi?"

"Maybe."

"Good answer. Okays, how do you like your kringle?"

Joshi wrinkled her eyebrows trying to figure out what *kringle* was.

"Oh no!!! Please, don't tell me you don't know!" Jÿger's pouty eyes grew watery as though he might sob, a sweet expression that almost melted Joshi's heart.

Joshi'd seen the word 'kringle' somewhere . . . she saw something about kringle on her character bio sheet! She took it out and looked at it.

"I prefer my kringle to be cold and to have it with hot chocolate," Joshi read straight from the text on the paper, as enthused as she would be if she were reading the morning weather report.

"Yay! Okay, that's-es it. You're authorized!" Jÿger jumped up and down and clapped his hands. Joshi still wasn't sure what the heck kringle was.

With that feat accomplished, Jÿger put a yellow dot sticker on Joshi's cheek. Joshi looked around and realized there was a yellow dot sticker on everything: countertop, Jÿger's pen, Jÿger's shirt, the wall, the ceiling, Jÿger's chair, and the neon scanner. Apparently Jÿger loved 'authorizing' things.

"So, Joshi. Do you have any questions?"

Joshi had a lot of questions about how she could get back to her old life, but she didn't even know where to begin. "Jÿger, do I have to memorize the papers in the folder to be myself?"

"No, nots at all. It should come to you naturally. You won't really need to look at those papers for a while, so you should keep them in a safe place, like a vault or file cabinet."

Yoshi glanced around the space behind her. Several feet away from **CONFUSEMENT CASES** there was another counter like Jÿger's, only it had a very long line of people waiting behind it holding folders. The sign above it said in small, squinty letters *Self Displacement—Psychological Conformity.*

"Hej, Jÿger, what are all of those people here for? Did they have character data changes too?"

"No . . . it's a sad story, reallys. These-es people come here a lot to cheats the system. They discards everything about thems—small personality-ish items, their values, ideals and imagination. All of its they discard for a chance at un-ultimate riches. It's ethically illegal here, but since the exchange is paper for paper, the clerk there bends-es the rules to get more business. It's delusional. Try going a day without having a favorite color, a hobby you do in your spares time, handwriting thats is uniques to you, a song you usuallys have stuck in your head, or the special habits you prefers for doing things in order by your owns way, or even going without a cravings for your favorites food."

Joshi looked into the waiting crowd. She saw no children there. There was a teenager, skateboard in hand, one with peeling paint and one wheel a different color from the rest, something that had comforted anger, revived lost energy, and traveled along everywhere. And that skateboard was to be given up, along with a pair of lucky shoelaces that never improved grades on test day but had been there to glow in the dark. A stack of papers detailing the hours of battle on a most-exciting videogame and the ambition to program a robot were to be dumped in a trash can as well.

A businessperson, fresh out of graduate college, stood straightening a tie that had been lovingly given to him by a best friend and worn to graduation with pride. In their hand he held the thesis that had changed a world perspective on poverty in third world countries. Both regarding effort and doing for the benefit of all, but if they didn't bring in complete monetary value, what good could any of it be to the owner? (Or so the businessperson thought).

Moaning about the long line was a yawning person leaving middle age and entering elderlyhood. What good had any personality done for a life, just getting one in and out of problems? Get-well-cards and photographs poked out of their folder. Problems weren't worth anything, money was. Why hadn't this idea come up before in their mind? Could it have really been that there were people and situations of no net worth that caused happiness? It couldn't have been. "I've lived this long and still haven't been rich!" was the tone of their grunting.

Joshi was disgusted. She didn't want to see any more of those people. She stared at the floor (which had a yellow dot sticker on it) and told Jÿger she would be leaving now that her character data changed had been 'authorized.' No sooner had she stepped outside was she greeted by a news kid. "Buy a paper! Papers let you read! The more you read of this, the more you can see!"

The kid lowered the stack of papers that they had been waving around, and Joshi realized it was not just some kid. It was someone with purple eyes and an additional set of eyes atop snail antennae coming out of their forehead. Joshi didn't know whether to run away or tackle Zippy and question her. If she tackled Zippy, Zippy might fade away again and it would hurt falling on the ground if there was no one to tackle.

Before Joshi could decide what to do, Zippy thrust a paper in her face, "The Zippedity Times." Its text looked like it might be written in Chinese. But the upper right hand corner had a line in English, "Somewhere, USA."

"I think it's time . . . . we had some . . . ." Zippy opened her mouth so wide that Joshi could see all of her teeth. And Zippy uttered that mysterious word, "KRINGLE!"

So...what is kringle?
Sometimes words create silence.
Character Data Center
The process of painting entails making new mistakes to cover up old ones.

Chapter 3

Between the earth and soul

Zippy led Joshi to an arcade a few streets away from the Character Data Center. The inside was filled with people, mostly preteen kids. Joshi statically shocked herself many times walking through the crowd. There were games of all sorts, ones that were sports, racing, mock gambling, fighting, puzzles, and shooting games. There was a machine with a moving basketball hoop that had footballs to score with. Mock-Slot machines gave out actual fruit from the winning combination of pictures, and an automated booth lit up with the daily high scores for "Smack-a-Germ" which averaged at—5 (probably due to the size of the whacking subject).

The featured fighting-style game was currently out of order, but the shooting videogame was popular, with several watching and cheering for the current player to defeat invading robots with a farting water gun. Another game was racing snails on a virtual screen. Joshi took special notice of this one because it had a huge yellow dot sticker on it.

Zippy motioned towards a flight of stairs behind what was quite possibly the world's largest pinball machine, which had buttons that could be stepped on and flippers as large as swinging doors. Its ball was larger than the tires of a monster truck and smoother than porcelain. Zippy and Joshi headed up a spiral staircase leading all the way through the ceiling, which, as Joshi could see was quite a ways up, perhaps over thirty feet. A handwritten sign taped onto the banister said, "Authorized person L's only."

On the second floor of the arcade was a small kitchen and stand-up bar.

"Wakezashi welcomes you and you!" A short girl with green hair stood by the door. Yoshi felt awkward, almost dizzy, as if she might fall backwards down the stairs, so she closed the door. "A Zippy and a Joshi, what great company for a rainy day!"

Joshi's first thought was *How did she know my name?* Her second thought was *I didn't know it had started raining since we came inside.* She did have a third thought, but she forgot what it was because Wakezashi started introducing her to someone else.

"Zippy knows Wakezashi and Rainer, but Joshi doesn't know. Hello, Joshi one! Wakezashi I am, and this," she said waving towards a boy behind the bar counter, "is Rainer, who is Wakezashi's assistant."

Rainer's hair was wet and he had water dripping from his clothes. He stood about three feet taller than Wakezashi, and wore a chef's hat and an apron that said, "Don't kick the cook. He is a Norweigan kung-fu master."

He showed them into another room where it was raining inside. Joshi and Zippy sat down at a table with a large umbrella over it that dripped onto the backs of their chairs. Rainer set down a dish of something edible and unrecognizable on the table. Zippy took a piece of the kringle and got down to business, and Joshi did the same, only they both had very different ideas of what getting down to business meant.

"What do you know about plumbing?" asked Zippy, pulling out a brilliant question to start a mealtime conversation. "Have you ever thought about experimenting with toilet paper?"

Joshi figured the more receptive she acted towards Zippy, the more inclined Zippy might be to telling her what she needed to know. "Plumbing is a system of pipes which may carry a liquid or gas, or in the case of videogames, people. Pipes are connected to different places, sort of like the entry of a wormhole in space, except that pipes are exact paths, not random. The last time I experimented with toilet paper was when I was out of notebook paper for taking notes on at school. I ran to the bathroom and got toilet paper to write on."

As chance would have it, this was precisely what Zippy was talking about.

"Yes!" Zippy outbursted. "You are correct in many assumptions, except that some pipelines are not as direct as you think. I have experimented with toilet paper as well, and I have also found a new use for it." Joshi hoped this 'new use' wasn't going to be for squeezing her brains out.

"When you faced a shortage of toilet paper when you were Yoshi, it was being used for experimentation. I was flushing the toilet paper to different places," said Zippy, "In time and space."

"Zippy, tell me how I can get back to who I was!"

"Why are you so impatient?" Zippy laughed. "Wait and see."

"I'm waiting as fast as I can," Joshi told her.

Zippy didn't look the least bit worried. "You are who you were, because you're you."

"No, in Tokyo!"

"Okay, chump. I'm going to do this like the cops do." Zippy whipped out of her pocket a flip-tip cell phone. You've got five minutes to make a phone call to anyone, anyone at all."

"I must call Hitoshi!" Joshi blurted. Why Hitoshi? Was it just the first name that came to mind?

The phone made beeped as Zippy dialed and she passed the phone to Joshi.

"Hello Hitoshi! It's me, Joshi! I just wanted to talk and to say . . ." Hitoshi yelled something in Japanese and hung up. Joshi heard a click and then Zippy's phone played its default dial message. "To make another call, start dialing. To call Mars, dial 1. To call Mercury press 3. To call outside of your network, the solar system, dial 1279734974785897559 8975. If you would like to make an interplanetary call, dial 101 and press the smiley face button.

"To stop hearing this message, reprogram your phone, make a call, take out the batteries, lock up your phone in a place far away, or turn off your phone. The connection waiting on line 2 is the CIA. The connection waiting on line 3 is . . ."

Joshi pressed the 'off' button in despair. How could he, Hitoshi, do that to his only friend? Hitoshi who had so faithfully served her udon each and every day and played go board games with her at school?

"I guess I would be upset too if someone called me in the middle of the night speaking a foreign language," said Zippy.

"This difference—it's like being a foreign exchange student, only I didn't choose to come here!"

"Which makes it all the more worthwhile." Zippy replied.

As they were leaving, Joshi thanked Wakezashi and Rainer for the kringle and Joshi asked Wakezashi how she had known what her name was.

"Your nametag—you keep it on your soul, between you and the earth, on the sole of your shoe." Wakezashi winked. She opened one of the kitchen cupboards and took out a recipe for chocolate chip cookies. "Ah, the ingredients.

Wakezashi needs jelly, onions, and some salad dressing for these cookies." Wakezashi smiled so brightly it looked like her eyes were giggling. "Come back in an hour or two and you and you can have some."

Chapter 4

The chapter that wouldn't end

Joshi and Zippy walked back down the long spiral staircase and into an empty arcade that had been crowded just minutes before. The herd of gamers would return the following afternoon during joystick rush hour. Joshi felt the incredible urge to play a game, to whack something or attack something or press lots and lots and lots of buttons. The noise and hustle of onlookers was gone, creating an environment for quality game play.

"Hej, Zippy, can we stay to play a game? I don't think the arcade closes for a few more hours."

"Oooh, I'll play a game with you! What type of game do you want to play?"

Joshi could hardly believe that Zippy was actually willing to do something that wasn't her own idea. "Well, I like fighting games best, but we can pick another kind since the only fighting game I see is out of order," Joshi said.

"Well, we'll have to fix it, then."

"Zippy, are you a technician?"

"No, but who ever said I had to be?"

That was a very good point.

They went over to the game titled "Go Ninja, Go Ninja, Go Ninja." Zippy ripped the "Out of Order" sign off the screen and pressed the 'start' button. The game's theme song started and Joshi didn't see what was wrong with it at first, or not until "Insert Paycheck" appeared on the screen. ^^^*Ninja* ^^^^*Ninja*^^^^^*Ninja* Joshi heard, the game song chorus that intensified in volume.

"If we play the game," said Zippy, "then I should be able to manipulate the corrupted .zip files that errorfied this start condition, which seems to be the problem."

"Zip files? Like the compressed files in computer hardware?" Joshi watched as Zippy spat on the screen and wiped it clean with her sleeve. The theme song restarted, and Joshi heard it more clearly now.

Go Ninja, Go Ninja, Go Ninja, Go Ninja, Go Ninja, Go Ninja, Go Ninja . . . Zippy sat herself down right on top of the game controls. *Fight Ninja, Fight Ninja, Fight Ninja, Fight Ninja . . .*

"Zippy files . . . files that go *zip-zip* . . . Say, have you got a paycheck on you?" Joshi shook her head no.

"What about an earplug?" Zippy asked, "Not even a thingamajigger!?" Joshi shook her head again.

Zippy stuck her hand into her right ear and pulled a pencil and then a piece of paper (both came out slightly covered in earwax). "You must go find an employee or official of the Character Data Center and ask them for a check."

Joshi was getting used to not asking questions about odd situations such as these. She ran out to the sidewalk and oriented herseld. The Character Data Center should be to the left of the poopy fire hydrant, her central landmark for orienting herself in the neighborhood.

She jogged past places with names and places without names, past places with people in them, and places without people, past people without places to be, and through and onto hard ground, light grass, concrete bubblegum messes, metal stones, clay mud, less people, more places, AND STOP! No people, no people, no people to be found near the place to be, which was . . . tug, push, *bang*, . . . LOCKED! She had been hoping to find Jÿger for this particular task since she knew she was less likely to feel embarrassed abound someone so strange, but now she couldn't talk to any other employee either.

Joshi passed the fire hydrant again, noticed it had been cleaned of all dog poop, continued walking, looked back and saw what she'd obviously missed in plain sight before, a sign. "C.D.C. staff will be back at work as soon as instant coffee machine can be repaired."

It seemed to Joshi that everything everywhere had impacts on everywhere else without even knowing it. It wasn't that things were broken and weren't bothered to be fixed, but more so that signs confused and explained at the same time. *Ignore every sign and you'll have nothing to live by, nothing to follow, nothing to do, nothing to be*, Joshi figured to herself (but not in numbers, in thoughts). She was reminded of singing snails.

Joshi felt something bulky in her right Yoshi boot. She reached in and pulled out a torn sheet of notebook paper. "50 km" was written on it. She turned the crinkly paper over to the other side, where it was written "Do not eat this paper. This paper serves a purpose. Until a purpose can be served, this paper needs be intact. Recycle wisely, or you might occur trouble."

Joshi knew her intuition just might be on to something . . . perhaps something with yellow dots. However, if this meant a certain accent-speaking, wrapper-chewing boy was 50 km of distance away, there wouldn't be much of a chance of finding him. It was, after all, just a videogame that was broken. Better go tell Zippy to fix it another time when there were functioning instant coffee makers to be found.

Joshi returned to the arcade. She walked past the pseudo-slot machines, past the Smack-A-Germ, and out of random curiosity she went around the far side of the pinball game, and almost running into . . . . Jÿger?

She'd gone so far when what needed to be found was so close. The snail-racing game was blaring with the squeaks of snails (what else?) amidst Jÿger's accompaniment of his own sound effects. '50 km Dash!' lit up on the screen as Jÿger jumped to the rhythm of a snail's slow plod against the background of fast-raving techno music. Joshi didn't want to interrupt, and it looked like it might take Jÿger a while to finish the round. She'd just have to wait. "Come on, Snail! EEEEEEE, EHHHH, EEEEE, EEHHH, aww . . . Turbo engine! Yay! I loves you, Snail-ee! My snails kick tails!" And it was over in less than a minute. Jÿger hugged the screen, pressing his cheek against it, off in a dream of pro snail-racing championships at grand racetracks, televised, bets being made, the press there to cover the action—Jÿger, in the spotlight, receiving the first place ribbon, all smiles, smiley, smiley, smiley . . .

Jÿger reached into his pocket for another quarter.

"Jÿger?"

Upon realizing someone could be watching him, Jÿger dropped the quarter.

"Oh, uhgs, hi, Joshi!" Hmm, there was something he was supposed to remember to do, now that he was back in reality.

"Hej, Jÿger. In order to fix a videogame, Zippy says you need to write a check. Could you do that for us?" Despite her efforts, Joshi did indeed feel embarrassed asking another kid for a check.

"Yapf! We justs need to gets a special kind of ice fungi to stamps on a check to make it officials. Only Data Centers personnel cans write specials non-cash, non-deposits checks like you guyses needs." He glanced around nervously, suspicious someone might be lurking in the shadows, waiting to spoil their secret fungi mission. "We need equip ourselveses with weapons thats will proves purposeful as we make our ways throughs the . . ." He lowered his voice to a gruff whisper. ". . . Fungi Forest."

Jÿger grabbed a mallet from the Smack-a-Germ game. The mallet's head had the consistency of stuffed animal filling. Joshi armed herself with the farting water gun from the shooting game. To commence the mission in full effect, Jÿger put on a pair of sunglasses and Joshi put on a clip-on tie she found in one of her shoes. Prepared for action, they ran out the door and around the back of the building to what Jÿger called a 'forest' of a few meters of trees, moss, and . . . fungi. The two agents from the arcade stepped forward into the mossy unknown, carefully monitoring the mushroom patch for suspicious activity. The trees were silent, the moss was for the most part motionless—well—actually completely motionless, and the fungi said nothing either. But the forest was not completely devoid of suspicion. Surely something was out there watching them pick mushrooms, something that disrupted the peace of nature.

From behind a tree hopped out a blue and yellow rabbit with one crooked ear. It approached Joshi and Jÿger with a quivering nose. The rabbit sniffed, and jumped three feet straight up in the air, perhaps out of excitement of meeting some strange new people. An orange collar around the bunny's neck said "Orange Fungus." It hiccupped, revealing its bright blue tongue.

Joshi wondered what was so orange about Orange Fungus. Orange Fungus was furry, small, and almost immune to gravity, but not orange. Jÿger picked up an orange mushroom and threw it a few feet. Orange Fungus bounded over and picked it up by wiggling its fuzzy spherical tail around it and swiftly carried the mushroom to Jÿger. Orange Fungus leaped once more, wide-eyed and waiting for something else to fetch. Joshi now saw that its eyes were large and orange. She picked up a green mushroom and threw it. Orange Fungus did not go after it. Jÿger threw a blue mushroom and Orange Fungus only yawned. Joshi threw an orange mushroom much farther than any she'd tossed before. Orange Fungus lit up like a light bulb and dashed after it as if magnetically attracted to it. With the bunny out of sight, Joshi and Jÿger resumed their mission.

Joshi scattered bits of yellow mushrooms Jÿger had picked to leave a trail behind them so they could find their way back later. The air got cooler and soon they found themselves in refrigerator-like conditions. The cold began to subside, however, when they came across a tree of epic proportions. Ice fungi filled up each branch and sprouted up like iced cupcakes. Joshi and Jÿger each grabbed a few to put in their pockets. However, they soon forgot about their mushrooms when they saw a house made of cookie dough nearby. Despite common sense, cavities and stomach aches waiting to happen, and the possibility that someone owned the cookie dough house, Joshi and Jÿger let their hunger get the best of them. They had bit off more than they could chew.

After the window shutters, door, chimney, and back wall had been dismantled and eaten, an evil nutritionist appeared out of nowhere. Her white sweater had a large carrot embroidered on it. She cackled and clicked her nails together as she magically captured the two children in a cage, lecturing them.

"Such bad children! Don't you know that the only food group for a balanced diet is vegetables out of a can? No more fresh veggies, bread and cheese, peanut butter, or cookie dough for you!" The evil nutritionist took out a can of green beans a foot tall. She tried to spoon feed Jÿger and Joshi vegetables, but she had poor eyesight, which enabled them to step back and let the vegetables fall on the floor. Jÿger swung at the evil nutritionist with his mallet, but it didn't help any because he couldn't reach far enough to hit anything outside of the steel bar cage. Joshi shot the farting water gun at the evilness, but soaking her in water did not melt the nutritionist, and the farting noise that came from it just annoyed her to the point of rage. "Two little boys, ripe to be eaten!" sang the cannibalistic nutritionist, who in her poor eyesight had mistaken Joshi for a boy.

Joshi and Jÿger cringed in fear. There wasn't much they could do now . . . They'd even tried telling the nutritionist that they had to go to the bathroom, felt like throwing up on her, had recently swallowed knives, and had poisonous venom in their bodies, but none of it convinced the evil nutritionist that they were less than tasty.

The nutritionist sharpened her knife and . . . .

WHAM! The remaining walls of the cookie dough structure caved in under the impact of an attack from a brightly colored bunny. Orange Fungus jumped onto the nutritionist and bit her, puncturing a hole in her head that released currents of hot air, and deflated her like a balloon until her rubber skin was just a torn shred on the ground. Orange Fungus gnawed through the iron bars of the cage and freed Joshi and Jÿger, who hugged the bunny and ran back to the arcade.

Jÿger used some of the ice fungi to write a check for Joshi for—7 cents. Joshi took the check to Zippy, who inserted it into the fighting machine. "Select weapon" appeared on the screen. Joshi chose to fight with a toilet plunger. Zippy selected a toothbrush. The two ninjas braced themselves for a fight over a go table. It turned out to be a fight that included playing the board game, go, as depicted on the screen with Zippy the ninja placing a piece on the board and jabbing Joshi's ninja with her toothbrush. *Go Ninja Go Ninja Go Ninja.*

Now it was Joshi's turn. She suctioned the head of Zippy's ninja with the plunger and threw her into the wall before placing her piece on the board. *Fight ninja fight ninja fight ninja.* As they entered their initials for a high score at the end of the game, Zippy manipulated the zip files. She reached into the machine and pulled out a coffee maker. "Someone will need this." Zippy's last adjustment to the game was to clear the list of high scores. "A real ninja leaves no trace."

Cling! Several coins poured out of the slot and a new message appeared on the screen: "Control your obsessions. A game should not be a path, but a rare event, Ninja." Joshi understood. People had obsessed themselves with games, and not stopped to live. The message continued on the screen "Ninja fighter, for every quarter you put in here, use a quarter to give away to someone who has never played an arcade game. A soul without sacrifice is no ninja." The last line appeared in squiggly purple letters: "Zippy was here."

Joshi and Zippy met up with Jÿger and headed to the kitchen upstairs for cookies. Jÿger remembered know what he was supposed to do—go see Rainer and trade playing cards with him. Rainer was collecting all varieties of kings (some of which were actually queen cards with mustaches drawn on them) and Jÿger was collecting all sorts of 7s (which included 9s that had been partly covered with liquid eraser fluid).

Jÿger introduced himself to who he called "the infamous Zippy in the blue," a great title for one who is not out of the blue but in it, and in an Abyss every moment. Because the world is connected in so many unrecognizable ways, things can change at a steadily inconstant rate, which makes life appear the same, as it should.

Wakezashi brought out her best batch of cookies, which were extremely delicious. Joshi gave her the left over ice fungi from the forest, which just so happened to be edible if prepared correctly.

"I don't know what trouble you had to go through to get these mushrooms," said Wakezashi, "but just remember, vengeance is sweet but chocolate tastes better!"

Joshi and Rainer joined Jÿger, Wakezashi, and Zippy sitting at the snack bar. Wakezashi turned on a TV. "Wakezashi's favorite TV show is on!" The program was a soap opera on the Ninja Channel. It was about two young ninjas, one was a girl with very long braided hair called "Yui, the master of kung-fui", and the other was a ninja of little expertise who was madly in love with her. His name was "Udo, the master of Judo." Jÿger and Zippy became particularly emotional over the thrill of the story and were in tears by the time the ending theme played. Wakezashi was quieting them down with tissues, waiting eagerly to hear the preview of the next episode. Jÿger informed the others about his adventure with Joshi looking for fungi in the forest.

Wakezashi laughed. "It sounds like something Hitherforme would do," she said.

"Who's Hitherforme?" inquired Joshi, unaware that she had just asked Wakezashi the one question that could keep her talking forever.

There is a difference between talking to someone and talking at someone.
Words!
[insert words here]
Sometimes we learn this the hard way...

CHAPTER 5

In the Realm of the Toilet

"Hitherforme," explained Wakezashi, "is a character in this book." She held up a book titled *3,000 Ways to Prepare Peanut Butter and Jelly Sandwiches.* "Oh, wrong book," and she held up another, *Famous Go Fish Players: Card Playing at its Finest.* "No, that's not it either. Wakezashi will find it later."

Rainer shifted his eyes away from the group. His frown and sunken eyebrows gave away his troubled mood.

"Is something wrong?" asked Wakezashi.

"I was in a fight against Raski the Dingo Dude when he insulted my award-winning mint pie. It just made me think that maybe my mint pie recipe isn't quite so grand as it is made out to be. I don't know how to deal when such a pansy no-good karate master threatens the undertakings of a skilled and courageously valiant chef."

"You have a deck of cards, right, Rainer?" Joshi asked.

"Yeah . . . ?" He raised one eyebrow.

"Well, get them out, and let's deal."

"Okay, then."

Joshi took the deck, which contained mostly kings, the cards Rainer collected. She selected a king that had a different back side than all of the other ones. The remaining cards she split into three piles: one that contained all number cards from 2 through 10, one with a small handful of face cards, and one with a large number of face cards. The selected king represented Rainer. The pile of number cards was his greatest works of food preparation, the large group of face cards was opponents in cooking and fighting, and the last small pile was his group of close friends.

"These all influence you directly for this problem. You know you have options: you can take your 'weapons' of your cooking talents to aid you in war against these opponents, you can take your friends to war with you, take both friends and weapons to war, call a truce by never attacking at all, or give Dingo Dude some of that awesome mint pie to taste," said Joshi pointing to a ten. Joshi went through each person in the pile of cards, their response to the situation, and what could be made of it. She then switched the roles and made Dingo Dude representative of the selected king card.

"What does dingo dude do besides fight?"

"He catches dingoes for pets."

"How many has he caught?"

"None."

"I see, so in retrospect he has zero weapons and you have many." She moved the number cards over into a pile of face cards and divided them into more groups. The conversation continued like this until all cards were sorted into piles of the same amount and Jÿger felt he knew exactly what he should do about the problem.

"Goodness, Joshi!!!! You took twenty minutes to deal out one deck of cards!!" Zippy didn't excuse Joshi's lack of shuffling skills, either, for when Rainer was satisfied with his decisions, Joshi picked up the cards and threw them all around the ground.

"To finish and prove your anger is no more, a fifty-card-pickup!"

Jÿger picked up three aces and gave them to Joshi. "You can start your own collection," he said, thinking about how Joshi was like an ace herself.

Zippy and Joshi left, saying goodbye to their friends, having had enough confusement for the day. Joshi headed to the place marked "home" by default in her mind, the building she'd woken up in who knows how long ago.

But, as two weirdos should know, enough is never enough, especially when it comes to confusement. On her way home Joshi saw a snail making its way down the sidewalk. It left a trail of snail ooze as an individualistic emblem of existence behind it as it proceeded courageously onward in the bold pursuit of life amidst the shadows of doom. The snail journeyed forth despite the possibility that might get smashed without it ever seeing its merciless attacker, all of which the snail must regard as a symbol of effort itself, for this was its daily life of adventure.

Or, as most others might see it and think it, there was a snail. It was on the sidewalk. It was leaving some yucky slime behind it. It was a snail and it was small. Being a snail, it would have to put up with being small its whole life. What was the ooze from it? Joshi said it was its own dignity of existence.

But Joshi's thoughts did not function the normal way, and if they did there would be no story, but just words describing a kid and a snail on a sidewalk without adventure and without anybody around to confuse by putting words on a page.

Why did it leave a trail of something behind it?

"Why is there so much thought pollution?" said Zippy.

"Why is it that I am the only one here thinking about snails?" said Joshi.

"Because you are the only one here who is thinking," replied Zippy, "and because you knew you were the only one here thinking at the moment, you knew you were the only one thinking about what you were thinking about. You knew you were the only one here who was thinking, because this place replaced by the pronoun *here* is in your head, and it is a place no one can be in but you, so you are the only one there, so you think and I say, and the only one capable of thinking."

"I forget that I am the only one *here*." said Joshi. "It seems like there's room for more, but how will I be sure because I think I'm the only one that's ever been *here*, but I feel like that's not the case."

Joshi glanced at the rather ambitious snail once more with her rather ambitious mind. "Every being leaves a trail, but it's not all ooze. My trail is made up of ink." The nametag on the sole of Joshi's boot had ink written on it, and like the rest of the shoe outline, made a light imprint on the ground it tread.

"Yet, Joshi, I do think you mean to say INK means something more."

"Exactly what? To say that I'm Not Krazy?" Because to say *I'm Not Crazy* was so out of fashion.

"Exactly that and exactly more."

Joshi walked into her default home and into her default bedroom with the default bed that was two feet too high, by default, and then over to where the file cabinet was placed, not by default, but by coincidence. Coincidentally, Joshi felt like opening the second drawer of the filing cabinet. If this was a world which held common sense as a virtue, Joshi would have had no reason to open the file cabinet because it would have appeared obvious and would have been assumed that the cabinet and its contents were undisturbed and the same in quantity as they had been since the last opening of the file cabinet drawers by Joshi.

"It seems undisturbed . . . but the inside is never blunt when the outside gives the whole image itself."

However, if you are like Joshi and like to state the obvious while investigating it, you know that there are no rules of common sense or common ignorance where Joshi stands in front of the file cabinet.

The drawer second from the top opened, having been yanked by Joshi's hand, an action obvious to you, but not to her. There was a new file in the drawer it next to her own "Joshi" one. This new file had a yellow dot sticker on it and said "Jÿger".

"Zippy, why isn't there a file on you?" Zippy was there with Joshi, but Joshi hadn't mentioned her being in the room because she thought it was too obvious to point out things like that in her mind.

"Hmm, look, there's a flying whatch'ama'callit out the widow." commented Zippy, having not stated there was a window because she wasn't sure it was obvious enough to those who were not in the room with them.

Joshi looked out the window and saw the airplane go by. Zippy hadn't said the whatch'ama'callit was an airplane because she thought it must be too obvious. But Joshi's thoughts remembered that there are those who are not in the room with them watching the whatch'ama'callit and explained in her mind what was obvious in her world so others would know. However, knowing doesn't always lead to the goal of understanding because not all thoughts are capable of being remembered, much less put into things people used to call "words" but are now called "thingadiggies" because Zippy, assuming the obvious was assumed, took the liberty of giving that thingadiggie her own specified synonym.

Joshi shut the filing cabinet drawer without reading the file about Jÿger. It was like a novel or wolf documentary she knew was going to be good and thus she put off reading till a specific relaxed time could be set aside for enjoying the indulgence of secret-keeping.

She yawned and decided to go to bed. Joshi pulled the comforter off of her bed and crawled with it underneath her bed, where she curled up into a ball, resting on her side with the comforter over her. At least this way she could not fall off the bed, she told Zippy. After hearing this thought from Joshi Zippy wanted to saw a hole in the floor for Joshi to fall through (so that Joshi could still fall out of her makeshift comforter-and-floor bed), but fortunately for Joshi Zippy decided against it. It was not common sense that stopped her, for Zippy did not live by common sense, but by her own common wit. Common sense would say that Joshi would get hurt from falling through the floor, but common sense did not know that there were resources in this place that would prevent that from happening.

The fact of the matter was that Zippy felt tired too, and took advantage of the space on top of the bed not being occupied. If there had been anyone to burst into the room at that moment, they might burst in laughing if they knew the background of a (former) dog sleeping on top of her (former) master's bed and the (former) master asleep under the bed, without Joshi even removing her shoes or jacket first as Zippy had done for herself.

Indeed, Joshi had not removed her jacket or shoes because she felt comfortable asleep with them on. Nonetheless, Joshi's right ankle hurt when she woke up. Someone was jumping on the bed and singing, "Good morning, Joshi. Good morning, Joshi. We're glad that you're awake, yay, yay . . . Good morning, Joshi. Good morning, Joshi. What will you do today, hey, hey . . ." As you may have guessed, that someone was named Zippy.

"Hej, just zip-it for a moment, Zippy." Zippy didn't stop singing but jumped off the bed and ran around the room looking for zippers. Joshi, usually a morning person, was not so much today. Joshi rarely ever slept because she seldom was tired, and her energy focused on important work that must be done for the sake of . . . something, she didn't quite know what. Having fallen asleep, and without doing important work first, Joshi felt she must have endured a phase of weakness. She resolved to make herself stronger by doing important work that day and remembering ambition, like the snail that could ignore the outward endangerments of society and focus on its duty. Joshi crawled out from under the bed. Her ankle hurt even more, but it was not twisted.

She felt inside the shoe on her right foot, finding something in her boot other than her foot. She pulled out a paintbrush, the Joshi paintbrush.

"The paintbrush of personalities," Zippy said, who stood over Joshi. Upon hearing the word 'paintbrush' in Joshi's thoughts she stopped unzipping the zipper on one of Joshi's jackets she'd found on the ground. Joshi held the paintbrush delicately in her fist, as if she knew what would happen next. From the base of the paintbrush the wood began to crack, letting out ferocious sounds of the wood splitting very loudly, as if a whole glacier was breaking and sinking away in the same room. The paintbrush held together without splitting into any pieces and only had a small crack on the surface that winded through the wood at the base and up a little more where it had cracked through the runic inscription.

Zippy was so nervous she looked as though her eyes might pop out of her head. "SO not good!! I have a problem with your problem! I don't know what your problem is, but it interrupts my problem with it, so just get rid of your problems so I can keep my own problems in peace!" She disappeared from the room and went into Joshi's head, searching for a sleep-mode button and not finding it. This intrusion of Zippy gave Joshi a headache. For a split second, Joshi saw a tail on her body. She saw her invisible tail as it would look like if it were not invisible. Long and fluffy with spots like a snow leopard's, it twisted around itself two times, coolish yet a bit lopsided. Joshi now knew why she had very poor balance, but she still did not know what was going on or how she would be affected by the new knowledge that she had a tail.

Realizing there could be no stop to this random occurrence of character growth and manipulation, Zippy left Joshi's head and walked in to the room again as though nothing had happened.

Despite Zippy's absence from her mind, Joshi felt a new sensation in her head. Muscles in her head were twisting. The paintbrush fell out of her grasp and she thrust her hands upon her head. An icy substance trickled down from her forehead. It did not occur to her that it was blood until a little fell off her hair onto her sleeve. She could not tell what color it was. She closed her eyes and saw inside her head instead of out. She saw her brain twisting and all of the colors that blended to make up her thoughts. Most of the colors she had never seen before and would never see again. Many of them were colors that did not exist in any rainbow. When her brain stopped twisting she saw blue, the color she normally saw when her eyes were closed. Joshi shivered.

She opened her eyes and saw the room just as she'd seen it before, only . . . different. Maybe the room itself was differentish (although it felt just the same) or maybe her eyes were what made her view of the room differentish.

On the floor sat Zippy with a monstrous, mischievous smile on her face. She clapped her hands and laughed. Joshi got the same feeling you have when you have a rip in the rear of your pants and no one has told you. Joshi stood up, had the same odd feeling, and sat back down, feeling just about the same, but perhaps not.

"Look at the bottom of your shoe!" Zippy giggled, falling over on her back and stomping her feet in excitement.

"Ioshi" Joshi read on her nametag. "Bummer. I was really getting fond of the way it was spelled with a 'J'."

Zippy led Joshi into the bathroom and asked her to look into "the mirror of water." In short, what Zippy meant was that she wanted Joshi to see her reflection in the water of the toilet.

Joshi looked into the toilet bowl impatiently. "So what does it matter if I haven't brushed my hair in a few weeks?"

Zippy shook her head and sighed. "That's what you get for not looking in a mirror very often. Take another look."

"Oh, my eyebrows are a little different."

"AND?" Zippy asked almost frustrated to realize Joshi probably could not recognize herself in a picture if she saw one.

"Oh, and my teeth are a bit duller, too bad."

"AND?"

"Oh, and I'm a boy now." said Joshi and she yawned . . . and then gasped. "What the heck? Holy peanut butter!"

"Joshi is a beautiful boy!" sang out Zippy, "No longer a handsome tomboy!

Ioshi looked, well, like he always did, in a state between reality and *here*, despite the fact that such a place might not exist at all.

"There is somewhere we should be, Ioshi," Zippy said.

"Uhh, where might that be?" Ioshi asked.

"Prepare for toilet travel, Ioshi! We must to the realm of the toilet go!"

They were there already in the bathroom, only not in the right state of mind.

Chapter 6

Be sure to flush before you leave

Zippy lovingly at her reflection in the toilet water and stuck her tongue out to make a funny face. Like a kid in a photo booth, she struck poses and admired herself, first with her tongue licking her nose, filling her cheeks with air to make them puffy, crossing her eyes, and wiggling her nose. After Zippy finished admiring her skills at making faces, she returned her attention to Ioshi.

"Just jump in. It might be easier if you go in feet first, but head first is more fun." Zippy stepped into the toilet. "Well, are you coming?" Without giving him a chance to respond, Zippy yanked Ioshi's wrist and pulled him into the toilet. He had put one foot into the toilet bowl when Zippy decided he was going too slow and took the liberty of shoving him downwards. He'd never thought a regular toilet could be big enough to hold one person, much less two.

The flushing sound roared louder than thunder. Slimey toilet water surrounded Ioshi and made his skin itch. He'd read somewhere that toilet water had an acidic pH. Ioshi remembered that once when he was cleaning a toilet the toilet water had surged up onto his arms and stung him with a burning sensation. This time, despite being almost completely submerged in toilet water, the water was not stinging, just itchy. The water that swirled out of the toilet was bright blue, as if someone had just sprinkled drops of food dye into it.

Ioshi knew he was underwater, but he didn't feel wet. He had to be underwater, though, because there was no surface to stand on and his movements were lighter. His nose was running, which always happened when he went swimming.

Zippy swam over to him and pointed upwards, or what seemed like upwards. Although directions are relative to the seer, there are times when even the seer can distinguish no direction. Ioshi thought he saw a snail swim by, but he couldn't be sure if he really saw it at all. Somehow it was harder to believe that a snail could swim than that two people could be flushed down the toilet. Ioshi had never been a snail himself, so he wouldn't know for sure if snails could swim. He'd seen snails flying in the air but not swimming around in a toilet.

The blue swirly water began to spin faster in large rapids. Something was coming from the direction Zippy had pointed to. It looked like a black bowling ball. As it came closer, Ioshi realized it was attached to some sort of pole or stick. Zippy grabbed the stick part of it with one hand, and was quickly dragged away. A moment later Ioshi felt something pulling at his head. He looked up and realized what Zippy had grabbed on to was a toilet plunger. The black rubber part of the plunger suctioned his head and sped upwards with him.

Before he knew it, Ioshi was sitting on his knees wet and cold in a toilet bowl. Zippy was crouched on the ground and leaned against the wall. She had one arm under her head which rested on the flat part of the commode behind the seat. "Zzzz," she muttered. "Z—z—zzz-z."

"Zippy?"

Zippy jumped up with a start. "Battle! Battle!" she screamed. "If we do not fight the fight, we cannot win the battle!" She woke up from a bad dream. In a calmer voice she questioned Ioshi. "Where did the battle go, Ioshi? Did it absorb you?"

"What battle?"

"*The* battle."

"I don't know."

"The battle," said Zippy, "is like a storm. It keeps traveling across the world and never ends. While it is sunny in one part of the world, it is storming in another. That is the way of the battle. The battle may be in one person and not another at the same time, no matter how close. A battle creates abnormal responses to normal situations. Battles can only be seen in the reflected image of one's eye or heard from the undertone of one speaking."

Ioshi wanted to capture a battle to discover exactly what it was, but he couldn't think on that at the moment. He didn't even know where he was.

"Where are we, Zippy?"

"In the past of your mind."

Zippy and Ioshi walked out of the bathroom and into the hallway of a building.

"This place is unfamiliar to me, Zippy. I've not been here before."

"Of course you haven't! This is Kristianshavn, Denmark, 1930."

"Then what's that modern toilet doing in that bathroom?"

"Only we can see that toilet."

"Zippy, Kristianshavn must still be a military base right now because it doesn't become a township until much later. How is this place connected to my consciousness if I've never been here? I would think it could be a DNA link, but I don't have any ancestors from this place because it's not a town yet."

"It is not necessarily DNA, but the information tagged to it. You have ancestors that came here during some point in their lifetimes. When you go somewhere, even just for a visit, it changes you, even by the smallest .0000000000763219%

of your being. When you are somewhere, you breathe the air there, walk on the ground, and feel the weather, just like any denizen would. Even these slight actions add to your conscious experience and will make walking on a similar surface, breathing air with the same scent, or experiencing similar weather familiar to you. Just one time is what it takes for a memory. The changes in DNA, like adapting to weather, are sometimes temporary in the person it happens to, but they reoccur later, even when the DNA strand is not in the same person because of the ability to replicate."

Much to Ioshi's surprise, they looked out a window and saw a small forest of bamboo. "They need bamboo for rigging ships, but I didn't know they grew it themselves."

"The condition of the bamboo plants doesn't look so good, so this project will probably be aborted soon and they'll resort back to importing. I wonder what will be done with the remaining bamboo that is no long enough for rigging? Do you know, Ioshi?"

"Bamboo can be used to make lots of stuff, I guess. It's especially cool for ninja weapons."

"I know a ninja that fights with a bamboo weapon," said Zippy. "Let's go take a look."

They ran down to the bamboo field. "Ioshi, I believe I know what will alert your senses of observation. If you change back to your regular form, you will be more aware of memories."

"You mean change back to my regular gender? How?"

Zippy shook a bamboo stalk at him. Ioshi fell down as a boy and stood up again as a girl. "You're not used to the rush of the change. It will knock the wind out of you the first few times, but eventually you'll get used to it."

Joshi noticed she had changed back to the female form of what Zippy considered Joshi's normal self, the light-skinned and yellow-haired. Joshi got caught up in thought she tripped over her invisible tail. Joshi fell down as Joshi and stood up as Joshi. No change. At least she knew now falling down wasn't the miracle in the transformation.

"Feel the bamboo leaves," said Zippy, "It's like you're holding the hand of an ill friend."

Joshi stroked a bamboo leaf and felt its cool dampness. It was like the nature in the water spoke to her. *I think water is my element*, thought Joshi to herself.

"I've never touched a bamboo plant before," said Joshi, "but I've used paintbrushes made out of bamboo stalks and wolf hair. My mom has a really nice bamboo brush that I will get to have someday."

"Joshi, it is this bamboo in particular that seems to have tied you to this place. The smell of it is in the air, the dew of it rains onto your fingers and the pebbled soil of it covers the ground, making this place very distinguishable."

"I can't smell the bamboo."

"It has a scent that slightly changes the air, even if you can't detect it. The bamboo-scented air goes into your lungs as you breathe and leaves a part of it in you, in your cells. Cells replicate and affect DNA, and then DNA replicates."

Joshi felt something was in her shoe. She took out the paintbrush of personalities. Its wooden handle was still cracked. She squinted to look through it.

"Zippy, could this be made out of . . ."

"Yes, it has bamboo hidden under the wood. It is your mother's paintbrush."

"But, wait! My mom's not Danish at all!! This does not add up!"

"Think about where bamboo comes from. Now think about where your mother comes from. Make sense?"

Joshi took a bamboo seed from the soil. It was something to be analyzed later.

Joshi and Zippy were back in the bathroom for another round of traveling. Zippy forced Joshi down the toilet in much the same way she had Ioshi earlier. As they were were flung back into the blue waters, Joshi heard words echoing towards her. "Dingo Dingo Dingo where are you you you? Come Come back back." Zippy swam towards where the sound was coming from and Joshi followed her. They found a distraught boy yelling about lost dingoes. As they got closer, Joshi realized that his voice was not actually echoing, but that he repeated random words naturally in his speech.

"Have you you two seen a dingo dingo dingo dingo? I seem to to to be stuck stuck here. I was was was looking in the toilet toilet toilet toilet toilet toilet toilet to see if there there was a dingo dingo dingo dingo hiding in there there.

Maybe a dingo dingo dingo dingo flushed me me down the toilet toilet toilet."

"Would your name happen to be Raski?"

"Yes Yes Yes. The the the dingoes must must have told you you you you. You are are are too too ugly to be a a a dingo." said Raski the Dingo Dude with an air of arrogance.

"And you are too mean for any dingo to want to be your friend. No wonder you can't catch one." Zippy threw back.

"Holy Dingo Dingo Dingo Dingo! You You You are so mean mean!"

"If you ever want to get out of here, you'd better be nice." said Zippy.

Raski wanted to get out of the toilet realm, but he didn't want to be nice. He stuck his tongue out at Zippy. Zippy stuck out her tongue and tugged the skin under her left eye for a major dis. Since Raski had refused the offer of escape by being mean, Zippy and Joshi began to swim away.

"Wait!!! Don't leave me here!" They ignored him.

"Don't leave me here, please!" Zippy turned around. Perhaps some bargaining could be done.

"So you're going going going to help me me me me me me?" Dingo Dude pleaded.

"That depends," said Zippy, "if you can pay in credit card or cash."

"But but but but you didn't didn't say I had had to pay the the first time time time!"

"You refused a good deal, buster. Hang up on a telemarketer and you'll regret not taking the first offer when they keep buzzing."

"I have have some coins coins in my my my my pocket. Will that that that that be enough enough enough?"

"How much is it?"

"Fifty cents cents cents."

"Not enough."

"Okay, so so so I really have have have seventy-five five five cents cents cents cents cents."

"Too bad. You're only a penny away from help."

"I've I've I've found another another penny penny. Please help help me me me me me."

"You were too late to take me up on my last offer, and since you seem to have more than one pocket full of money, taking into consideration that every five seconds a new coin magically appears in your pocket, I'll issue you one final fee with no taxes involved. 1,000 dollars. Give it here or remain here forever."

"Just just wait a few few few few few minutes minutes. I know know know I should should have have have at least half half that amount!" Raski the Dingo Dude started turning out all of his pockets and shaking his pants madly. At least five pounds of coins floated in the water around him.

Zippy held back a laugh. "No, no, no, my friend, I was joking. Just swim around in an upwards direction to get out of this place. Avoid any blue toilet plungers and look for a dingo-ish one to get to where you need to go."

Zippy and Joshi took off again. "One more stop before we return," said Zippy. Before Joshi could wipe her runny nose they were being plunged up into a new adventure.

Zippy and Joshi were shot out of a toilet as if they'd been shot out of a cannon. Both rocketed up and over the stall of the toilet they'd came out of and hit the mirror on the bathroom wall simultaneously. They slid down the wall onto the sinks. The whole room was covered in graffiti.

Two tough looking teenagey girls jumped down from the top of the stall doors where they had been sitting, watching Zippy and Joshi's arrival. "H-i, space, Z-i-p-p-y." said one.

"Have you come to talk or have you come to practice fight? Do you only have one friend with you?" said the other who used normal speech.

"I have one friend with me. She is Joshi. She is a ninja that fights with a bamboo paintbrush. We have come to practice fight. I was hoping you could tell us more about her weapon."

"We shall see. It depends on if the paintbrush chooses to reveal itself. If not, I will not be able to estimate its ability." She introduced herself to Joshi. "My name is Fjordka. Qrsis is a younger friend of mine, although you cannot tell she is 10 years younger than me because she is three inches taller. We are both robotic units, as you may have figured out. Qrsis has a programming error and can only spell what she says. I may speak fine, but I cannot count or do any sort of mathematical problem, no matter how simple."

"E-n-o-u-g-h, space, s-a-i-d. L-e-t-'-s, space, f-i-g-h-t." said Qrsis. And they did. Qrsis led with a fierce charge at Zippy, which was narrowly dodged. Joshi was about to punch Fjordka from behind when she jumped around quickly and kicked Joshi onto the floor. Zippy picked up Fjordka and bodyslammed her once, but it didn't seem to faze her at all. Fjordka's kicks were more powerful than Zippy's bodyslams and headbutts. Qrsis jumped from stall to stall and Zippy jumped from toilet to toilet in a frenzy. With one arm grabbing a sink faucet for balance, Fjordka was able to kick anything within a wide range. Joshi could punch and bodyslam well enough with people her own size, but by no means did she stand a chance against two older-looking and sturdier opponents. Joshi was about to punch Qrsis when Qrsis fell to the ground without being touched. Fjordka dropped Zippy from her headlock position and ran to Qrsis.

"She needs batteries." said Fjordka, pulling out two double As. She opened Qrsis's mounth and reached her hand down Qrsis's throat, stuffing in the batteries as if they were food. A few seconds after the batteries were swallowed, Qrsis woke up.

"Joshi and I must be going now," said Zippy, "but I will want my fight back!"

Back 'home' Joshi planted the bamboo seed. It seemed at home in its own pot. The seed was at peace, but Zippy was not.

There is a difference between bad dreams and nightmares.
I don't know what it is.
Sometimes I feel very, very small.

CHAPTER 7

Who reads chapter titles, anyway?

"I want my fight back!" screamed Zippy in an almost squeaky note of frustration. "If a certain someone wasn't too shy to show off their paintbrush weapon, I might not have this problem!"

Joshi sighed and looked out the window, wondering why the sun wasn't blue. If the sun was blue, the blue light wouldn't hurt her eyes. Blue light would turn the grass aqua and tree trunks a dark gray. It was summer in blue's winter, or so it seemed, and summer was a daze to Joshi, who was left to her own devices in a territory of few resources. It was unlike the school year when materials could be acquired from the local dumpster. But it could not be summer if she was not where summer had visited her before. Joshi looked at the small little pot where she'd planted the bamboo seed.

Bamboo would be green in the yellow sunlight. Joshi sat down on her two-foot tall bed. What was the point of having a tall bed, anyway?

"★Swipe★ ★Glug★ ★Crash!★" Joshi was tumbled over onto the ground in an instant. She should have known that bed would continue to be dangerous. Whatever it was that had exerted force on her ankle was still attached to it. Joshi stood up and as she took slow steps she dragged out the rest of the creature who had been under her bed. Zippy's hand wiggled around her ankle. "I want my fight back!" she whined without letting go of Joshi's ankle.

"What were you doing under there, anyway?" Zippy pulled Joshi's boot off of her and looked into it, and then pulled it over her head for a closer inspection.

"I am looking for something very important. I thought you might know where it was."

"What are you looking for?"

"I don't know, but I will know when I find it." Zippy took off the boot and made a sympathy face. "So, will you help me look? Please, Joshi?" Zippy whimpered.

"Where do you think it could be?"

Zippy rolled her eyes. "Oh, I don't know. It's somewhere in the universe, I suppose."

A deep, gurgling sound came from the bathroom. It had the effect of a helicopter landing in water, lots and lots of water.

"Whatever it was, did you flush it down the toilet?"

"Oh No, no nonononnonononono! I forgot to flush the toilet! I bet it's clogged now."

Joshi ran towards the bathroom. It didn't make sense to her that a toilet could be clogged without anything getting flushed down it, but at the very least she should make sure the toilet wasn't about to combust. Her hand was on the bathroom doorknob, ready to turn it, when . . . .

"Don't go in there, Joshi!"

"Why? I've plunged toilets many times. I'm used to toilet duty."

"Oh, an expert! Well, okay then, unclog the toilet!"

⋆Whoooosh!⋆ Joshi had just stepped in front of the toilet when a wave of water crashed into the wall and flooded the floor, leaving behind a soaked Joshi with a plunger in her hand. Joshi set aside the foot-long plunger. She had a feeling it wouldn't be much help. More specialty equipment would be needed.

"Zippy, bring me a bigger plunger!"

Zippy tiptoed up to the bathroom door and stuck her hand into her ear and fumbled around (her ear was alien, large and hard to ignore, like her voice). She pulled out little by little a handle that extended from inside her ear. With one last tug it snapped with a popping noise. Zippy's ear's waggled from the vibration of the suction. At the end of the handle was a three-foot long stick with a rubber plunging apparatus at least three feet in diameter.

"Super plunger!!!" Zippy proclaimed, naming the weapon to increase the awe of its power. Joshi plunged up a storm with it, but after lightning struck the bathroom counter five times the toilet was still very clogged.

"A bigger plunger!!"

"One large plunger, coming right up!" shouted Zippy. "Would you like fries with that?" she added.

"Um, sure."

"Super Mega Plunger!"

Zippy produced an even bigger plunger and pulled some French fries out of Joshi's boot. Joshi took a break to eat the fries before continuing. Joshi pounded and plunged and stood on the plunger like a pogo stick and jumped up and down in the toilet, but was the effort was futile.

"A bigger plunger!"

"Super Mega Jumbo Plunger!"

Joshi plunged with all her might, yet it was not enough. She plunged like there was no tomorrow, and still the toilet was clogged. Joshi wasn't about to give up, though.

"Zippy, a bigger plunger!"

"Super Mega Jumbo Gargantuan Plunger of Whirlwind!!!!!!!"

The last plunger lived up to its name and sent a blast of swirling toilet water at Joshi. She heaved the plunger out of the toilet with a ⋆pop⋆, at the same moment suctioning out a potty-traveling visitor.

Orange Fungus bounded forward with one happy leap into Zippy's arms. "Fuzzy Friend!" Zippy greeted the rabbit, stroking its colorful fur. She twisted its ears together and turned them. The rabbit began to shrink with each twist of its ears. It didn't seem to mind, though, for it patiently sniffed Zippy's hands as she continued. When she was content with the size of Orange Fungus, Zippy set the fuzzy one inside a Yoshi boot on the floor that had fallen off of Joshi during her plunging mission. Orange Fungus snuggled up in the coziness and looked quite content in its new comfortable surroundings despite Joshi's bad foot odor.

Joshi walked out to the hallway and pulled open the first drawer of the file cabinet. Unless the Abyss was held together with duct tape, she'd need to get it from a source other than Zippy's enlarged ear cavity. The file cabinet might offer a clue, if anything else . . . but not in this drawer. The top drawer was now a habitat for wild snails, as it read on a sticky note in front of snails, snails with puppy dog paws, faces, ears, and tails crawling around in an environment of mushrooms and rocks. She closed the drawer, and wondered if it was necessary to even look in the second . . .

"Joshi! Orange Fungus just burped . . . and he made some other noises too. I think he needs some toilet paper."

Duct tape or no duct tape, something needed to be done about the toilet. Joshi didn't want to risk it clogging again. Joshi sloshed around in the swamp life, feeling the dampness in her one soggy socked foot. She wiped some leaves off a lump on the wall and thanks to her awesome luck she uncovered a roll of toilet paper. Zippy took a strand of it to clean up after Orange Fungus, and Joshi wrapped the rest of the roll around the closed toilet seat and the base. She felt quite satisfied with her defense plan. No more toilet storms, swamp invasions, or toilet visitors. Orange Fungus yawned, and something round rolled out of its mouth, a half used roll of duct tape.

"Yo, I was looking for some duct tape earlier." said Joshi, disappointed that the weird coincidence hadn't happened earlier.

Zippy's eyes sparkled as she spoke. "Looking for something? Oh, yeah, I'm looking for something!"

Joshi decided to ignore the slush on the ground and sat down next to Orange Fungus. She understood that sometimes messy is just another normal state of life.

"Thank you for the duct tape, but may I please have my boot back?"

Orange Fungus hiccupped.

Zippy's eyes widened. She sat down next to Joshi and looked into Joshi's ear.

"No, Zippy, whatever you're looking for, I'm sure it cannot be found in my ear."

"No, Joshi, I've already looked in your ear for what I'm looking for," said Zippy, "But what I see right now is blue earwax!" The blue tips of Joshi's hair were slowly extending, and Joshi's complexion was fading also. Her eyes went to a dark gray, the color of a tree trunk in blue light. But where was the blue light coming from, and why only Joshi? "Because Joshi is a fragment of the Abyss!" whispered Zippy into Joshi's ear. "You will be called into the Abyss when you are 100% confusement in your identity . . . confusement, such a normal state . . . the Abyss is not a bad place, but it is . . . . where all forgotten thoughts are dumped . . . and some details . . . are better not remembering . . ."

Joshi wasn't paying attention. "Please, Orange Fungus, I need my left boot because it has my nametag on it!"

At that moment they heard a big bang, not one magnificent enough to start a universe, but one that was followed by a painful "OUCH OUCH!" Another bang made the wrapped-up toilet seat jiggle a little and then ripped off a few layers of toilet paper around it. One more bang shook the floor. The toilet lid snapped free of its toilet paper restraint and swung upward. Joshi was very annoyed to see her defense system destroyed. She should have taped it shut instead.

"Well, it might as well break open because I was wondering how we'd ever use the toilet again with the lid tied closed," said Zippy.

First a head and then an entire person emerged from the toilet's murkiness. Raski fell out of the toilet, head first into the swamp water on the floor. "Yuck Yuck Yuck! Nasty, gross gross, and muddy muddy muddy!"

"It is not yucky, gross, or muddy in a swamp." corrected Joshi. "The 'yucky-nasty-gross-muddiness' you see looks brownish because it is colored by the leaves of a plant used for making tea." Zippy scooped up some water into a mug, stirred sugar into it, and began drinking.

"So so it's not not dirty dirty dirty?"

"Yeah. Without the leaves, the water would be clear. Otherwise, it is the perfect home for tiny infectious microscopic creatures and animals such as leeches, snakes and alligators," said Joshi.

Zippy spit the water out of her mouth and poured what was left in her mug back onto the floor.

"But but no dingoes dingoes dingoes dingoes dingoes live in in in swamps swamps?"

"No."

"What did you come here for anyway?"

"Well, I'm I'm I'm chasing chasing a din-" Raski stood up awkwardly. His knees were taped together with duct tape. "YOU YOU YOU YOU DINGO! I'll get you you you! How dare dare you you you you duct tape me me me me!" Raski pointed at Orange Fungus, who hopped out the door, still in Joshi's boot. It had a roll of duct tape in its mouth. Raski the dingo dude pursued the rabbit through the hallway, running with his feet pointed inward. Only the lower half of his legs were moveable. He almost looked like he was doing an odd dance as he made clumsy circles waddling on his feet. Orange Fungus, on the other hand, was faster than a hyper hamster on an exercise wheel. Raski picked up more speed when he discovered it was easier to hop with his feet together, but couldn't catch up to the bunny named after citrus-colored fungi.

"It would seem that Orange Fungus duct taped your knees so that you would have to hop like he does." Joshi observed. "It's like being in his shoes, only he doesn't have shoes so he's in one of mine."

Raski, not having an ear for phychology or a mouth for one either, didn't listen past the first sentence Joshi said to him. "Dingoes dingoes dingoes don't don't hop!" he said.

Orange Fungus hopped out the front door of the building. Raski followed, also hopping, but he soon fell down with a crash when he opened the door. An unconscious Jÿger lay on the grass where Raski had accidentally tackled him in his attempt to catch Orange Fungus, who bounced up and down by Jÿger's side (still in Joshi's boot), concerned for him. Jÿger had a package under his arm, the reason he'd been at the door in the first place. A girl with pale blue skin and dark blue hair anticipated Zippy's aid to the fallen one. She took off a sock from her shoeless foot and waved it in front of Jÿger's face, hoping the smell would wake him up. When it did not work, she put back on the sock, which itself had not been blue for a moment but was blue again. The kid tried to speak, but her tongue was blue. Zippy said that giraffes have blue tongues, but giraffes were not of the Abyss. But the one of the blue could not hear her. She saw blue from hazeled blue eyes and heard blue from the beat of blue blood pumped out of her heart. *One shoe foot, one sock foot, one shoe on, one shoe off, one mind thinking, one mind not . . .*

She remembered something she had never known or forgotten. If the visual message could be given in words, it might be somewhat like this, but like any translation (this one being from sight to words) some tiny details or feeling is lost from the total effect. *The earth is a world of places, and not a world of people. People have forgotten that the world they exist in is not a world of people. People belong in places, but places are not dependant on people. Animals live in a world of places, but people often think in a world of people, a world that is obsolete to the function of the universe. You used to not know that you were a person. You have forgotten this.* The blue kid received the whole message, but no one else could without being in the Abyss the exact moment as she.

And then the memory of the remembering faded, almost forgotten as if it were a passing dream. Joshi was no longer the blue kid. She was still there, sitting on the grass. She had both of her shoes on. Jÿger the snail jockey laughed. Rainer and Wakezashi and Orange Fungus were there too but she didn't see Raski anywhere.

Zippy ran around excitedly. She waved a pair of pants in the air. "I've found it! It was where it was, and I knew it would be there!" Zippy cleared her throat. "Attention, all of you. A new fad has come in from where it has come from. Something old and grand and new for you and you and you and you and all of you!" She took a moment to point at each one of them. "It's called 'lederhosen!'" Zippy pointed to the lederhosen she wore and the pair she held high in her hands. "Your tall bed is good for something, Joshi. It's good for finding things." Zippy cleared her throat again. "So I am inviting all of you to Joshi's place where Joshi will have everyone as guests on her own live talkshow! And, without further ado, I present to you the sidekick of the lederhosen industry, Lederhosen Boy!"

Raski walked out proudly wearing lederhosen in his outfit. He carried a huge bouquet of flowers and seemed to be enjoying himself, perhaps too much. Zippy's eyes spun as she went on about how she adored boys in lederhosen.

Jÿger handed Joshi the package he had with him when he was knocked out. "I'm supposeds to delivers this to you, yapf." he said.

"Are you feeling better now? You must have been hit pretty hard."

"Yapf. Orange fungus broughts some funky tastings fungi that wokes me up. You were staring offs into space ats the time."

"Raski told him getting tackled would only hurt if he was conscious, and lucky for Jÿger he wasn't," Zippy said with a giggle.

Joshi was curious about the package.

"It must be something that you haven't lost yet," said Zippy. "You've found it ahead of time before you lost it in the first place.

Warning:

Do not plan on using a bathroom after reading this chapter. The author is not responsible for strange and unexplainable phenomena that might occur. If any living mold, slime, or member of the animal kingdom crawls out of your toilet, please either call an animal protection agency or check to see if you've taken all of your mental medication. After writing this chapter, the author went to the bathroom and inadvertently clogged the toilet. The author then took a plunger to it and did not go to bed till the toilet was unclogged, around midnight. This was the same cursed toilet that was used once by the author five years ago and subsequently pumped forty gallons per hour at the expense of the person paying the water bill. The toilet almost fell through the ceiling when a leak was too late to be stopped. To avoid such complications with the unflushable portions of travel, try walking to your destination instead. To avoid complications of being hurt on the toilet when fighting, don't fight in a bathroom. To avoid complications of injury by use of toilet for doing business, get exercise by digging a hole behind a tree and fertilize a new habitat for snails.

A true statistic from research discovered by the journalism teacher of the author: an average 40,000 Americans were reported to have injuries from contact or use of toilets in the year 2004.

CHAPTER 8

Sincerely but not sincere

While the group enjoyed the non-blue weather outside, Joshi opened the package Jÿger delivered. It was from Wakezashi. Joshi pulled a book out of the box. Its title was The Legend of Hitherforme. "Thank you, Wakezashi!"

"Wakezashi's pleasure. Wakezashi knew Joshi would get it sometime."

Joshi opened the book. *Once upon a time in the World of Nevers there lived an invisible hedgehog. Also in the World of Nevers lived a girl named Hitherforme. By the way, the hedgehog had nothing to with Hitherforme, but telling about a hedgehog is a great way to start a story.*

"Joshi!" Joshi looked up. Except for Zippy everyone else had suddenly vanished. "So, have you drawn up the battle plans, yet, Joshi?"

Before she could begin to wonder what Zippy was talking about, Joshi responded, "Almost. I have it all mapped out in my head and I just need to put it on paper. The strategy consists of three fronts, one in the World of Nevers, one in . . ."

"Excellent! We shall have the troops surrounding them before they can even whistle the alphabet backwards." Zippy saluted her and marched off.

Joshi did not know what sort of pretend-game was starting, and she didn't know why she'd played along when she had no clue what Zippy was talking about . . . or did she? A troop's plan to surround a battle? No, a battle plan to surround troops. Weird it was that she had mixed up the words she meant to say in her thinking. It was like the spell-check for her brain was not there to filter unnecessary typos in her thoughts.

Joshi walked inside where Zippy sat at a table flipping through a stack of papers. "What does you now, Zippy?"

"Writing letters to all of my chumy-chum chums. Looks like you've gotten some letters of your own to read in your pocket inbox," she said and pointted to Joshi's cargo-pants pocket, which bulged with a crumbled paper ball inside it. Joshi took it out and unfolded it, hoping for a message from the place in Japan she used to call home.

Instead the following message was written in blue ink:

Dear Joshi,

There is a videogame console in the file cabinet. You can play if you plug it into a tree. Maybe we'll go one-on-one. If not, we can always duel later.

Love Zippy

"Why don't we play right now?" Joshi asked.

"Well, you see, I'm splendidly busy right now." Zippy hummed as she flourished her pen to make large cursive letters on the papers where she answered her mail.

"Oh, well then I'm going to go take a walk," Joshi said, *and try getting a way out of here and to Tokyo,* she added.

"Well, if you're going to do that, can you deliver these letters for me along the way?"

"Sure. I will make sure your correspondence with our allies is not interfered on my ninja mission." Joshi spoke cheerfully as if she was . . . home, and there forever. Forever. Forever is longer than infinity. Infinity lasts until there is an end. Forever lasts as long as there is never an end to the end.

Joshi's hands were full of stationary Zippy had not told her not to read.

Dear Rainer,

:)

Love Zippy

Dear Wakezashi,

Don't forget to take the french fries out of the freezer in twenty minutes. By then they should be hot enough to store in my ear for tomorrow's tea time. Please also tell Rainer to turn over the piece of paper delivered to him. There is writing on the other side of the blank sheet.

Love Zippy

P.S. Have you seen Joshi anywhere?

Dear Raski,

You are a dingo-head and your poetry sucks. Your socks don't stink enough, and I hate your guts.

Love Zippy

Strangely enough Joshi met every single person she had a letter for right outside of her house except for Qrsis. Even more strangely enough such an occurrence was hardly strange at all compared to the other strange things she had encountered. She went back inside and opened the second drawer in the file cabinet. There was a videogame console, three files, and a deck of playing cards. Joshi equipped the deck of cards in her cargo pocket. Perhaps they would be of interest to Rainer.

Her walk down the street was eventful. A group of little kids were counting down the seconds till the stoplight on the corner changed from red to blue, someone was correcting the spelling errors on the "stopp" sign, and a squirrel was munching on a small bit of watermelon growing on a tree. Joshi looked in the window of a toy store where she saw a big, bright sale sign with a pogo stick under it. The pogo stick was a lively blue hue (hey, that rhymes!) with special non-slip-grip handles and a meter to keep track of how many jumps had been taken and the precise number of miles that had been jumped with it. A glossy tag advertised that the pogo mechanism could reach speeds up to fifty miles per hour.

Joshi gasped when she saw a reflection in the glass over the pogo stick. For a split second she saw herself as she used to be, the Yoshi Tokio with her rectangular ears, smug grin, and shoulder-length black sloppy hair that stuck out of a backwards baseball cap. The Yoshi Tokio image was unlike Zippy's alteration of it that had large, almost conical ears, neatly-trimmed pigtails, and a perky smile. In an instant the image was gone again and Joshi didn't know if it had even actually been her in the shop window glare or the image of a passerby that may have looked faintly like the way she used to that had stimulated her mind to believe it was the embodiment of a past personality.

Joshi began to walk away, but she was stopped by an odd sensation in her left foot. In her boot was a cap, but not just any cap. It was *her* cap. The cap that she once wore with the Joshi boots but did not match it even though it did very much belong with it. She put it on and looked back in the window. Seeing a normal reflection of herself as Joshi, she was relieved and disappointed at the same time. Joshi smiled at the gray and yellow pogo stick under the sign. "As it was to be, only as it should have been now and was not then . . ." she whispered to herself, patting herself on the head where the Japanese embroidered on the cap showed in the reflection. Japanese? She could feel the outline of letters on the cap, spelling something, something like T-R-O-P-S . . . in Western calligraphy. The reflection was not so normal after all.

Ditching the nonplussed confusements of self-identification mental crises, Joshi ran on to the arcade. A piece of gum was stuck to the door and it made Joshi's hands stickyish. Some of the gum rubbed off onto the folded letters she was carrying. She couldn't read the names on some because of her smeary red fingerprints. She opened one to see who it was for.

Dear Qrsis,

If the paintbrush of personalities is activated again soon, it is likely to emit an ekko particle. If that is to happen, I believe code runaroundandpaintem shall overrun the serotonin levels and devastate the later cause. However, if the serotonin assimilates into the form of runaroundandpaintem, equilibrium will be saved, but the weapon itself may shatter inside out. If the serotonin does not bounce back in a runaroundandpaintem form, I will certainly need your help in taking every ounce of adrenaline out of Joshi's mind through conjugation. The adrenaline levels in Joshi are already overwhelming. Giving her a headache will subdue it for now, but later I will have to take more drastic measures.

Love Zippy
P.S. I want my fight back

"So, that's what this is, an anti-Yoshi plot to wrack my head for some freaky alienistic battle plan." Joshi thought. She stuck the suspicious letter back in her pocket. Joshi didn't exactly feel like seeing anybody face to face after finding out that the entity which had started as a painting in her sketchbook was now plotting to take control of her mind . . . or why hadn't she figured that out before? Before . . . when Zippy was the wacko troublemaking tour guide to 'the Abyss' that took control of her former life . . . and was now possibly targeting her present one? Was this a game? Or a fight? Joshi smirked. "It's my fight, and no one can take it from me." Games . . . like the ones she played with herself, or the invention of Zippy where the rules are made up as you go . . . She could play a game with herself right then.

Joshi took the game console from the file cabinet and plugged into a tree behind the arcade. A screen popped up out of the machine, and the following words appeared: "When does Z come before Y? In the Zippy and Yoshi Game!" Joshi sat down facing the console and began to play. The screen showed two little kids playing a game about pretending. Both wore Japanese-style school uniforms. One was shorter than the other with large round mousey ears and light lavender eyes. She wore a bow on the collar of her shirt and had ribbons woven into her skirt and shoes. That character laughed and made lots of noise.

The other was silent and opposite in her appearance with the kerchief of her school uniform tied in a loose half-knot under the collar of her shirt. She wore long socks and shin guards and in place of a skirt she wore shorts with a wavy hem, and her boots were made for rain and snow and were certainly a few sizes too big. This one was coloring a connect-the-dots page and scribbled randomly because she could not see the smiley face her lines were supposed to connect. The noisy one turned to the quiet one and said, "Let's pretend we're butterflies!" The other one said, "No, let's be wolves!" They argued with each other until they agreed to be samurai on a secret mission in outer space.

"What freakish characters," Joshi thought. Her stomach rumbled. She could go for a sardine sundae right about now. Then she realized it was her video game character whose stomach had made the rumbling noise. Her stomach shook when the game controller shook her hands.

Joshi was losing horribly in the game at first, but when she stopped looking at the screen she began to win quite easily. How did she even think that would help? Randomly pressing buttons without knowing what was going on. Somehow it worked. An unusual tactic, but a good plan. Plan? A battle plan? What was she thinking? Joshi already had a battle plan—a plan to capture a battle. It was as plain and simple as quantum physics. Joshi prepared a response to Zippy's letter. Zippy was supposed to be her friend. She was meant to be an ally. Alien or not, *canis lupis*, a kid's best friend could not forsake someone who wanted a friend. She signed the letter with the line *Sincerely, but not sincere, Joshi.*

Zippy was still her friend and would be until things changed, Joshi planned. If her moment in battle failed, she would have to face Zippy's moment, and she did not even know what it was Zippy's moment was to be, although it was described in the letter she read that was addressed to Qrsis. It was not Joshi's right to read it, but it was her right to fix a mistake by looking at the name on it. But she had looked beyond the name and at her own, written where she thought it didn't belong. It was not Zippy's right to take Joshi's former appearance and drag her far away, but it happened. *Who is this kid/dog/alien?*

This inconclusive resolution left one conclusion. "I must know what Zippy knows. And where she is, I must be there too. If I am where she is and she is not where I am, I . . ." *will have to stop being in many places at once*, her thoughts finished for her.

Meanwhile, Zippy folded the paper of her last letter. This time she made it into a paper airplane. "All done!" She clapped her hands together in delight, trying to maintain her usual optimism. She was not sad and she was not angry. She was concerned. Lederhosen might cheer her up. "Rask-iiii! Raski-doodle-doo! Raski the dingo dude!" She yelled, looking around. "I want my lederhosen marketing campaign! I want to make big bucks off of this lederhosen business. Call up Wall Street! Call up the Hang Seng! Call up every stock market on the planet! We're going incorporated, so spill the ink, but I'm not krazy!" She finished yelling and then remembered what she had been thinking of before. She could go for a cheese-fondu sundae right about now.

Zippy leaned over the bamboo pot on the window ledge. The little bamboo looked thirsty. Zippy put a straw into a glass of water and stuck the other end into the soil of the pot. When no water had moved, Zippy used Plan B. Plan B for this situation, as was Zippy's Plan B for everything, was to write a letter.

Dear Little Bamboo Plant,

Please drink water. Water is good.

Love Zippy

When the bamboo plant did not read its letter, Zippy would have used Plan C, but she didn't have one, so she turned to Plan D. Plan D stood for "decorate." Zippy searched her memory for pictures. When she found some good memories, she looked frame by frame at her photographic memory. When she had decided on a few standstill shots, she reached a hand into her ear and pulled out a roll of film. "I should go digital next time." Zippy ran into the closet where it was nice and dark. Twenty seconds later she came out with a stack of photos in her hand. She propped up the photos in a display around the little bamboo plant. There were photos of herself and of the bamboo forest in Kristianshavn, and of Orange Fungus in Joshi's boot. She took one of Raski in Lederhosen out of the pile and pulled at it till it stretched to poster size. That one was for the marketing campaign.

Zippy resumed looking at pictures and placed one of Joshi next to the bamboo plant. It was her favorite picture. It showed Joshi and no background because Joshi was the only thing in that specific memory. Joshi wasn't capable of happiness, was she? But Zippy, Zippy wasn't capable of sadness. And the little bamboo plant was not capable of drinking water through a straw. Water streamed from Zippy's eyes, but she was not crying. She made her eyelids function like faucets. The water rolled onto the bamboo plant where it splashed off of leaves and soaked into the soil. Zippy patted the bamboo plant. "You know what? Joshi—she fights an invisible opponent. Oh, and it's not her tail I'm talking about."

Unexpectedly, Joshi came running out of the bathroom. She was breathing hard. "I can face adversaries with my Ninja-berserk skills," she puffed, "but there is one I fear" ⋆cough⋆ "waiting for battle in the bathroom." The bathroom door tilted open slightly, emitting a formidable glow.

CHAPTER 9

Find a problem for the solution

Zippy, armed with an invisible weapon unknown to man (in other words, nothing) charged into the bathroom full speed, as dangerous as a sleepy koala ready to attack fresh eucalyptus leaves. She roared and she squeaked, and she thrashed all around, until . . . until there were suddenly no noises to be heard coming from the realm of the toilet. Zippy spotted what she was looking for. Joshi backed away further from the bathroom door, hoping that the monster that lay within had not gotten to Zippy. If worse came to worse, she hoped that Zippy could escape down the toilet, if the threat emanating was too great to bear with the heavy weight of an invisible sword that could not beat the agile swiftness of the haunting beast looming before her.

"Hang in there, Zippy! If you can, try digging trenches for defense! And never show your back to the enemy!"

More chilling silence followed, and Joshi grew more anguished by the second. *I'll have to seek revenge for this!* she thought, looking for weapons of invisible destruction. *If I don't hear anything in the next five seconds, I'll run in there. 5-hope I don't have to do this-4 hope I don't have to do this-3 hope I don't have to do this 2—hope I . . .*

"Heee, hee, hee!" giggled Zippy. "What fun!" Zippy came out. Her hands were clasped together, hiding something. "See, Joshi?"

"Nooo! It's gonna get me! Zippy, quick, run!" Zippy had released the ladybug from her palms. As it appeared, such a "monster" had no intentions of fighting at all.

Blood rushed to Joshi's eyes, reddening them. The ace of ninjas drew a card from her pocket, stuck it between two crossed fingers and whirled it across the room in unnecessary defense. The card sliced into the wall and stuck there, challenging the silence that rang out from its impact. Joshi threw another card, which scraped across a countertop before cutting through a plastic recycling bin. Soon a row of cards grazed the surface of the ceiling and clanged on the half-closed window blinds, some slipping through the space between plastic shades and shattering the glass of the window. In a last ditch attempt to subdue the nearly forgotten enemy to certain doom, Joshi threw a card diagonally in no particular direction, spun in a roundhouse posture as she turned. A hand reached out and stopped the movement of the card with a pinch of the thumb and pointer finger, delicately snatching the paper card out of the air. The card was a king of diamonds. Rainer stood there holding it. "Sorry to interrupt your destructo-thon, but there is something that requires your immediate cooperation. We have a problem. The sky is falling."

"The worst kind of natural disaster for this time of year—all year round, that is." said Zippy. "When did you notice the skyfalling had started?"

"Wakezashi and I were just depickleizing pickles—Wakezashi has this wonderful kudzu plant that grows delightful pickles—and so we were in the kitchen depickleizing them into cucumbers, and because the depickleizing fluid smelled, we opened the windows. I had put suds and dishes in the sink earlier to soak, and when I went to wash them I felt sharp pieces of something in the water. At first I thought a dish must have broken, but then I realized that bits of sky were falling through the open window above the sink. That was about five minutes ago."

Joshi felt an unusual silence in her head. The next thing she felt was her body hit the floor. Her conscience was not in her head. Maybe it never had been. Her thoughts were not in her but far away, as if they had always were. The words and feelings connected to her body, though it lay eons away in a different dimension. Joshi saw through her eyes and felt through her skin, but it was like being in one place and watching through a camera that was miles away. And suddenly her connection to earth was suspended, and Joshi forgot that there was somewhere else she was supposed to be at the same time.

She was reminded of the pain of the mind and of the pain of the heart. Her soul had a body that it did not own, but needed. A soul does not rest inside a body, but follows it. When she remembered this, she came back from the Abyss, and part of the Abyss followed her back.

Joshi woke up to an adorable gray puppy licking her face. She was at Wakezashi's place (hey, that rhymes!). Zippy was asleep nearby on the floor, hugging one of Joshi's shoes. The puppy licking Joshi was of the Wolfie breed, Wakezashi explained, a new breed made by a paintbrush in the Abyss that used Joshi's thoughts as paint. Joshi petted it. "What's your name, Wolfie?" A computer cord extended from the puppy's ear and plugged into Joshi's. A small stream of data in the form of digital DNA rushed into Joshi's ear. Joshi felt all warm and fuzzy inside, like she had just come indoors from a blizzard and was wrapped in a furry blanket drinking hot chocolate in front of a fire. It was the kind of feeling of what it is like to be a furry little creature with a tail and a sense of undying loyalty.

The puppy barked. "My name is Lukkar," said the puppy Lukkar. Joshi could understand the little dog's language now that they had shared DNA memories. He twitched his ears and wagged his tail. Lukkar blinked his eyes. One was blue like a dog's and the other was yellow like a wolf's, both cute and fierce. Joshi saw how content he was and wondered if she should feel the same way. After all, now both things she'd ever wanted had been granted to her—a best friend and a pet dog.

A piece of sky tore through the window and hit Zippy on the head. For the first time since she'd become humanish, Zippt poofed into her blue-purplish dog form and walked over to Lukkar. Her steps were unsteady and random. She muttered while sleepwalking. "Wow, Joshi, you've really changed, and lots."

Joshi patted the dog-form Zippy on the head. "I'm right here, Zippy, and I haven't changed," she reminded her.

"Um, Joshi . . . I wouldn't say that . . ." said Rainer. "Your ears look rather long and pointy, and—hej, I can see your tail!"

One shoe on, one shoe off . . . said the void inside the Abyss, but Joshi didn't hear it; she was laughing.

Rainer pulled the curtains more tightly around the windowpane, but in the process a piece of sky tore through the curtains and gave him a paper cut on his arm. He gave up on setting up a boundary in front of the window and sat down. His complexion was pale and his eyes looked droopy.

"You need some water," said Joshi. She ran to the cabinet to get a glass. There were many sorts of odd cooking equipment on the shelves she looked through, including an ice cream melter and square-ended spoons. Wakezashi's silver and porcelain spork collection shone radiantly in one cabinet, and another held measuring cups for baking ingredient measurements such as one-hundredth of a teaspoon, thirty-thousandths of a cup, and twenty-nine hundredths of a liter.

When she did find where the glasses were kept, she took one over to the sink and turned on the faucet. Milk poured out of the faucet into the kitchen sink, and that was no good. She turned the faucet to the right some, and out poured soda pop. Another turn and lemonade came out. When the faucet was turned all the way to the right, water came out. She filled up the glass and gave it to Rainer.

Meanwhile, Zippy was still in her dog form and had twisted up her alien antennas while stumbling around. Still sleep-walking, and she yelled, "Oh No! Don't flush the earth down the toilet!"

Joshi reached for her boot on the ground. *One shoe on, one shoe off . . .* As she put it on, her paintbrush fell out. Something red rubbed onto her hand when she picked it up. At first notice she thought the paintbrush was bleeding, but that didn't seem to be the case. The other possibility was that it was paint. Hard to tell, really, since both paint and blood can be different shades and thicknesses. The blood—or paint—bled out of the crack in the wood of the paintbrush, which had grown larger and branched off into smaller crooked lines like the branches of a gnarled tree. Joshi's name was still visible on it in runic, but she didn't know that the next time she saw her name, it would be carved in a different font style.

Beams of sun began to shine through the kitchen window curtains. The light grew brighter and soon Joshi and her friends heard no more crashing bits of sky hitting the walls outside. Wakezashi came in with a chocolate-covered cheesecake. Zippy poofed back into her humanish form when she smelled its home-baked awesomeness. Each person ate a piece, but when Lukkar whimpered for some, Joshi said she didn't think a dog should eat food unhealthy for it.

Zippy clarified the situation. "It is okay for little Luk to have some, because, like myself, he is a special situation. He has obtained some human DNA, copied from you Joshi," Zippy stuck out her tongue, "If we can call you a 'human'—you're more of a werewolf or wannabee shape-changer. So, a small amount of human DNA would allow a 3 month old pup like Luk to digest foods such as chocolate with no harm done." Zippy was of course the authority on canine behavior; her puppy personality changed more often than the toilet flushed.

Lukkar took a bite of cheesecake. "Cheesecake is good," he whispered.

When the cheesecake had been finished off, Lukkar went outside to pee and when he came back he dragged in with him a large piece of sky. "The sky is good," he said. The piece of sky was in very good condition, and since the sky has special properties other materials do not, Wakezashi and Rainer agreed to keep the piece of sky in the storage room at the arcade because it might later prove useful.

In response to the unexpected sugar from the cheesecake, Lukkar fell asleep in the hood of Joshi's jacket. Zippy had a completely different response. She was bouncing off the walls, literally.

"How 'bout we take a day or two off today, Joshi?"

"What do you mean? Haven't we been goofing around ever since we got here?"

"Yeah, and having done such important work, why don't we spend the day relaxing?"

"Uh, 'kay, I guess . . ."

Not many people know Zippy's definition of a "day off", and even those that do are still trying to figure it out. A lot of people know Zippy—more than—20, which is how I can comparatively say that lots of people know Joshi. Quite a record, for a fragment of imagination like Zippy, that is.

"Let's go rate toilets," said Zippy, and they certainly did. Zippy dressed in a pleated skirt and short blazer and blouse, and she made Joshi wear a plumber's jumpsuit. After walking several blocks, they arrived at an office building where they walked into the lobby up to the front desk. Zippy, carrying a briefcase, presented an I.D. as Official Inspector of Restrooms, and to Joshi's surprise, gained access to every women's restroom in the building without being doubted or ignored. They set to work and cleared every stall on the first floor.

Each toilet that passed inspection was given a rating in star stickers pasted on the stall door. Ones that didn't pass were given a frowny face drawn in blue marker. They went to many bathrooms in many buildings in town this way, being doubted by none and respected by all. Some toilets were "tested" as they felt necessary. In other words, Joshi drank a lot of ginger ale along the way, and the rest of their method you can read in between the lines of what I'm talking about.

Joshi and Zippy sometimes left messages hanging above commodes or even drew pictures on the toilet lids. They were not breaking rules—Zippy was an official of toilets, and she would be slacking off on the job if she didn't do her (self-proclaimed) duty.

When they got bored of the same old inspections, they decided to take a side trip to Europe for "business travel"—business, indeed, in more ways than one. In some public places they got free access to otherwise costly bathrooms, ones in which normally a fee must be paid before you are let through a revolving door into a hallway of locked doors that are really small toilet stalls.

Each one of these toilets passed inspection with flying colors as bright as the decorated toilet paper provided with them. Some European toilets had foot pedals for anti-germ flushing, and some were pipelined so confusedly that it took a good search to find the handle that flushed the toilet, be it above the apparatus or on the wall near it. Joshi and Zippy also went to parts of China where individual restrooms were already rated by tourist bureaus, but not individual toilet stalls. Zippy taught Joshi to use the eastern style toilet, which was more efficient and hygienic in design, and in some cases the advanced eastern style toilets allowed more of a group discussion to take place in the ladies' room.

Zippy and Joshi did not stop there. To campsites and to port-a-potties they went. Somewhere along the way Lukkar woke up and joined their game with his inspection of trees and fire hydrants fit for the dogs' business. "Trees are good," he said. Some outhouses received 5 stars, the highest rating. They put up signs in the woods that marked good places to dig holes for emergency-gotta-go situations.

"We have collected excellent data!" said Zippy, scribbling on paper she held on a clipboard. "We must see how a bathroom stop changes the mood of a person."

With that they went back to their own town where they had started their grand adventure and stood in a hallway at a local fast-food place near the restrooms. A yellow dot sticker was on the sign of a door that said "men". Hardly a moment passed until the stick-er of yellow dot stickers came by. Jÿger walked into the bathroom looking kind of mellow. "I gots to thinks of somethings . . . I's must thinkses of somethings . . . What cans I do? . . . What wills I's do?" he muttered on his way in. A few minutes later, Jÿger burst through the bathroom door in a much better expression. "I's gots it! I's gots it!!" he almost yelled in excitement, so happy that he could kiss a toilet seat out of joy (but he didn't do that).

"What we have just seen," said Zippy, "is a dude walk into the bathroom and come out a new man!" Zippy herself had another idea. "Would you like to change into boys and go check out urinals?"

"Urinals are . . ." Lukkar began to say, but Joshi stopped him.

"Naw, that's okay." said Joshi.

"You sure?"

"Really, it's okay. I think I've had enough relaxing for one day."

Zippy laughed. "Then you mean you have some work to do—places to go and people to meet."

"I don't want to meet people."

"And I don't want to meet aliens," said Zippy with her tongue sticking out of her mouth.

"Aliens are good," said Lukkar.

"I can't guarantee that you'll like every one of them, but eventually you'll be forced to." explained Zippy, "and you can get acquainted with the first one right now." She pointed to a mirror on the wall.

Two saber fangs that hung down past her chin and two soft puppy dog ears that poked up out of her hair were definitely the most noticeable changes Joshi recognized in herself, besides the fact that her eyes were creepily colored dark blue where they had been white and a light gray where they had been red. Her feet felt very springy, as if she could jump five feet in the air. "Say hello to the id of your brain, Psycho Lurid. Typical, impish id, that one."

Then Joshi was shifted back into her "normal" Joshi form (which still had the elf ears and visible tail that emerged earlier). Suddenly she felt very stiff, fragile and unable to move quickly. Joshi closed her eyes and saw herself standing in the room she was in, and she saw a little kid run through her as if she were a ghost. The kid looked to be about four and teetered and tottered, rolling on the floor, a bit dizzy from jumping around. The little girl took hold of Joshi's foot and looked at the boot on it. She accidentally spat on it as she giggled in delight. She poked the nametag on the shoe sole and then let go of Joshi's foot and sat alert. The looked around as though she heard something. She then fell on the floor and curled into a fetal position, snoozing away with a stuffed gray dog in her arms.

Joshi soon heard wonderful music, like a dog whistle, but deep and melodious. She began to feel tired too. "This," said Zippy, "is your cerebrum. She takes up many nicknames, but you think of her as Pokey, the nickname you used to have in elementary school. Her 'dog' is Runaroundandpaint'em. Sometimes a fake tail has to be pinned to her in order for her to have better balance." The little kid's image faded away and Joshi returned to "normal," if such a word could be used to describe anything about her anymore.

Zippy and Joshi were walking home when they met up with Jÿger. He didn't smile or tell any jokes. Jÿger turned to Joshi and stated in a monotone voice unusual for him, "Zippy has located a battle. A consuming, warping, dangerous, fascinating, exquisite phenomenon. It's inside you. And half of the human population where you are from. But your battleground expands beyond their universe." One part of Joshi's mind wondered where the "s"s had gone in Jÿger's speech; another part didn't even notice the change in Jÿger's speech patterns because it was seriously contemplating the importance of the message. The Ioshi part wasn't thinking at all; he only saw how cute Lukkar was as he slid across the ground with the tag of Joshi's boots in his teeth as she walked.

Joshi ran. Her spirit ran faster than her body and it took her farther than her eyes could see. What her eyes could not see, her intuition could.

Chapter 10

Mir ist Schwindlig (Me is dizzy)

Zippy was dressed in lederhosen, ready to begin making fashion fans sick to their stomachs. She had been walking home with Joshi when they saw Jÿger and stopped to talk.

"Oh, Jÿger, do you like my outfit?" beamed Zippy.

"Thoses are nices shoes, Zippy, very, uh, spiffies."

"But what do you think about the lederhosen?"

"Very . . . interestings . . . uh . . . very Germanish-es."

"Oh, yes, they are very German. Would you like to model a pair? Boys don't try a trend until they see girls wearing it first. Right, Joshi?" Zippy looked around. "Where to did Joshi go?" she asked Jÿger.

Joshi wanted to run away. She wanted to see home, the home she'd came from in Tokyo. She could run forever and still not get there. After realizing that Joshi went to the only home she had, the house where Zippy visited her. She ran upstairs to the kitchen for a mug of hot chocolate to calm her down. She prepared instant hot chocolate and sat on the window bench of the kitchen window. The pot next to her on the windowsill, held a little bamboo plant that had not yet sprouted. Without any profound thought about anything, Joshi looked out the window for a few minutes and then got up to rinse out her mug. She glanced at the bamboo pot again and saw that the plant had sprouted.

Undoubtedly, she'd witnessed something very important. The bamboo sprout was blue, which reminded Joshi of that word Zippy liked to say over and over: abyss. The little bamboo sprout began to shrink back under the pebbled potting soil, and Joshi felt like she was going with it somehow. Her vision followed the bamboo into its roots and back out of the soil into open air. Joshi looked around, seeing the kitchen exactly as it had been before, except that it was all blue now, even her hair and skin.

"So this must be the Abyss." Joshi said out loud in awe. The little bamboo plant nodded and waved its little stalk.

"The Abyss this must be so" echoed the bamboo.

"Can you talk?" asked Joshi.

"In Abyss the must only can here talk."

"Maybe if I read to you, you'll be able to talk more understandably."

"That me not maybe help is read not speech talk with change."

"Well, it's worth a try, isn't it? Even if you can only talk in the Abyss." Joshi took the Hitherforme book that had been lying on the kitchen table. Its cover, like everything else, was blue here, and so was the text inside.

"I've been reading this book. Right now I'm on chapter ten. 'After Hitherforme defeated the grabbysnatchers of doom, she went to a friend of hers to see if she could borrow a dragon.'"

"Dragon luck good brings," said the bamboo plant, "You dragon no claws with having spirit be."

"Wow, that's deep and philosophical, like a quote I would write down. Explain some more about this dragon with no claws theory."

"Claws four dragon have when does, in place society royal above is signifies."

"Oh, so a dragon with four claws is reserved as a sign of royalty."

"Claws three dragon nobility to belong. Claws two dragon for peasants the is."

"So a dragon with no claws has no place in society. Do you know that you can see real dragons without leaving the earth dimension?"

"No. Place be in I Abyss that so can I. Of I little in earth know."

"There are three species of dragons on earth. Each represents a different element, but they all represent the fourth element, fire, because that's what all dragons come from. There is the dragon of the wind and sky, and it's also the dragon of light and dark and of air. It is called a dragonfly. Dragonflies are very fast in flight and often live near swamps. There is a swamp in the bathroom, so maybe one day I'll catch one there and show it to you. Dragonflies are the smallest of the dragons. Hundreds of thousands of years ago, dragonflies were much, much larger and had wingspans up to five feet long. Even in that time they were not the largest of the dragons, for several many more dragon species were on earth at that time too, and some were larger than we can possibly imagine. A dragonfly, though associated with the wind, starts its life near water.

The second kind of dragon is the dragon of the earth. It is the largest of the three dragons, about 7 feet long and very plump, but not nearly as large as the dragons that lived thousands of years ago. It is scaly, but does not have the same type of scales as does the dragon of water. The earth dragon is as lazy as the dragon in Chinese zodiac folklore, and like in the folklore, it is very dangerous. It can kill a person through a bite. It has sharp teeth, but its teeth do not do most of its killing; the bacteria in its mouth does. This dragon, known to some as the komodo dragon, must crawl everywhere it goes because it does not have both wings like the dragon of the sky.

The third species of dragon, the dragon of the water, has neither legs nor wings and only tail-like fins to move about with underwater. It lives in extremely deep places underwater and it is small, but slightly larger than the dragon of the wind. I think it is the most wonderful-looking of any of the dragons, and it is very rare. Marine biologists have named it the sea dragon, and it shines like a piece of coral. I think it keeps so deep underwater because it is very shy like I often am, and it also has secrets to keep. If it were to swim farther up in the ocean, it may fear telling its secrets, or that's what I think."

"Dragons I like," said the bamboo plant, using the best sentence structure and word order of any of his dialogue yet.

"Dragons are good," said Lukkar, who had been quietly listening from Joshi's jacket hood.

"I wonder if there's anyone who doesn't like dragons. I could check the file cabinet." Joshi left for a moment and came back to the kitchen window. "When I looked in the file cabinet, there weren't any new files on anyone I've met, but there was an empty file that had blank papers inside and no name on the label. I brought Jÿger's, because it's been in there a while and I still haven't read it. It's not nice to go looking into other people's personal business, but it seems like I'm supposed to read them because they are in my house in my room. I don't think they would say anything mean about a person anyway. Besides, you guys aren't going to tell anyone, I mean, a puppy and a bamboo plant wouldn't tell anyone."

Lukkar shook his head no, and the bamboo plant, which Lukkar and Joshi named Emune, made the same gesture by shaking his tiny bamboo stalk.

Name:	*Jÿger*
Occupation(s):	*Character Data Center Employee, Delivery Boy, Maintenance Worker for the town (trash management)*
Favorite Color:	*yellow, aqua green*
Hobbies:	*playing videogames, chewing gum wrappers, daydreaming, singing (when he's in the shower)*
Bloodtype:	*A*
Pets:	*a bat named Skweekers*
Extra Notes:	*Currently his will states that everything in his 'estate' is left to someone named Orange Fungus. Three years ago, at the ripe young age of 11, he lost 100,000 dollars in a snail racing bet and still today is working hard to pay it off while supporting his pet bat and his younger cousin, Imp.*

Lukkar licked Emune. "Wait you be till I person-form in am," said Emune as he shook off the slobber.

"Really!? You can take a person-form?" asked Joshi.

"Might if try I enough hard to."

"Can we see it now?"

"For tomorrow wait. I to energy up build that for."

"Alright. I think we'd better go back to our world that isn't all blue. Do you know how?"

Emune wiggled his stalk into the pebbles of his pot and brought them back to the colorful world they came from. Only Emune was all blue in both places.

"Jooooo-shiiiiii!" yelled Zippy. She ran to Joshi and hugged her. "We've looked all over for you! I've missed you sooooo much! We've done everything together and I didn't know what I'd do without you!" Zippy put her hands on Joshi's shoulders and shook her in attempt to act very sentimental. "Remember the time we fought in the Trojan War together?"

"Um, yeah, sure."

"Those were great times, weren't they?" Zippy's eyes sparkled.

"Oh, of course they were."

Zippy hugged Joshi tighter. "And it was genius of you to come up with that horse idea!" Zippy gave Joshi a small slap on the back. "Remember when we built the pyramids?"

"Sure, Zippy."

"And when we won the American Civil War? And when we were the first to land on the moon? And when we won the Iditarod? And when we got gold medals as a bobsledding team at the Olympics? And when we discovered Pluto? And when we invented the radio, now that was teamwork! Or when we climbed Mt. Everest in record time? Or when we wrote a bestselling book? How 'bout the time we were the first to reach the North Pole? Or when we discovered a new species of fish? Or when we cloned a sheep? Or when we were knighted by the Queen of Denmark? Or when we saved China from invaders? Or when we . . ." Zippy could go on forever with her list of friendship activities.

"Zippy, I want to go back."

"Me, too! I miss the Great Wall and all of the beautiful scenery, and the amazing opera theatres with elaborate costumes, the yummy food, the excellent indoor and outdoor plumbing—"

"No, Zippy. I want to go back home. To my home, where I was before I got to this place, whatever this place is called."

To Joshi's surprise, Zippy's smile did not fade and she did not sound angry as she would have a few days ago when Joshi had just arrived and had wanted to go back. "If you wanted to leave, you should have just asked." Zippy took out her official clipboard and scribbled on it as she had when inspecting toilets. "For how long will you be absent? I must write you an excuse so that you are not counted tardy for your talk show appointment."

"Talk show appointment? That wasn't a joke?"

"Nope. Today's the day for it. So, how long will you take your leave?"

"The rest of forever."

Only then did Zippy stop smiling. She forced her mouth into a smirk, shook Joshi's hand, and saluted her.

"Then so long, see ya."

"One more thing, Zippy. Can I take Lukkar and Emune with me? They could communicate back and forth between us."

"No, yo-yo. It's an all or none deal."

"Goodbye, then, Zip-Zip." And Joshi was no longer there. She was Yoshi, and she was standing outside of the comic office where she worked. A "For Sale" sign hung on the door, which was locked. It started raining as she walked home. Yoshi walked up three flights of stairs to the floor of the apartment building that her family lived on. She could hear her whole family from down the hallway. They were arguing, yelling, screaming, tearing apart each other's moral values. Someone would be angry because her boots were wet. Someone else would be angry because she had not taken an umbrella with her. Someone else would be angry because her scalp was bleeding all over her cap, which meant it would have to be washed thoroughly. Someone else would be angry because she had come home just in time for dinner.

Yoshi removed her shoes and got the courage to open the door. As soon as she did she wished that she hadn't. Her relatives were angry at her and she couldn't tell whether it was because she had been missing or because she had come back. Yoshi collapsed on the floor, her mind full of headaches.

I wish I could go back, she said in her mind.

For a moment she thought she heard Zippy's voice: *If you want to go back, then all you have to do is ask.*

Yoshi felt her mind going away again. She opened her eyes and her headache ceased. Several friendly people were around her and they all seemed concerned. She suddenly realized that she didn't know any of them. She must be dreaming, she thought, because a girl sat in front of her that looked a lot like herself and she had some strange green snaily eyes poking out of her forehead on antennas. She realized her hair wasn't as long as it ought to be; she didn't feel it brushing against her cheek. She was still wet . . . *wet from what?* She wondered. Her shoes were missing, but she was in someone's home, after all, so she had probably taken them off.

"Joshi's nametag is not here!" said the look-alike girl in front of her. The look-alike girl went to another room and came back a moment later with a pair of boots. "Please put these on."

"You're not joking, are you? I mean, this is your home and all, right? . . . Oh, maybe you mean for me to leave now! I'm so sorry. I don't know how I got here!" The girl who had forgotten her name stood up with her boots in hand.

"No, please, put on your shoes . . . so . . . so that your feet won't be cold."

"Yes, thank you." The girl put on her shoes and remembered who she was, who she was with, and where she was. Joshi remembered going back and coming back, and she remembered forgetting who she was.

"Yay! Joshi's back!" Everyone (Raski, Jÿger, Zippy, Wakezashi, Rainer, Qrsis, Fjordka, Raski and two people Joshi had actually never seen before, although they both looked familiar) cheered.

"Yay is good," said Lukkar, who had climbed back into Joshi's jacket hood.

Zippy brought over a girl with a dragon perched on her shoulder and Joshi tried to figure out where she'd seen the girl before.

"This is Hitherforme," said Zippy, and to Hitherforme she said, "Joshi's been reading the book about your adventures."

Joshi was stunned to find out Hitherforme was a real person. Meeting people from fictional books was something she'd never experienced before, even in Zippy's wacky world. "Nice to meet you," Joshi said.

Next to be introduced to Joshi was a boy that looked familiar to Joshi because he looked to be the same age and height as Zippy and looked a lot like her. "Is this your brother?" asked Joshi.

"No."

"Your cousin?"

"No," said Zippy smiling even wider, "This is someone you already know. This is Emune," said Zippy, "and he's going to wear lederhosen." she added quickly, leaving not just one but two people with surprised looks on their faces.

After getting over the shock and confusion of trying to figure out how in the world a bamboo plant could look related to an alien dog turned human, Zippy pulled Joshi aside.

"I know there's something I didn't tell you, and I apologize. This place is called the World of Nevers," said Zippy. "I didn't tell you that from the start because I wanted this place to seem more realistic."

No matter what you call it, it's never going to feel like reality, Joshi told herself. "Zippy, did you warp the real world to make it worse than it is so that when I went back there I'd immediately want to come back here?"

"No, I promise you I didn't. When you saw your spot of relief gone, the comic office, you saw the rest coming. I do want you to stay here and be safe with friends you'd never have elsewhere, but I won't lie to you, because I am your best friend and your ex-pet dog, and that requires loyalty."

From the other room they heard everyone say in unison a startled, "Ohhh!"

"RASKI SAID HE DOESN'T LIKE DRAGONS!"

"YEAH YEAH YEAH? WELL, WELL, SO WHAT WHAT?"

"I need to keep an eye on that Raski!" said Zippy. Joshi watched from the doorway as Zippy snuck up behind Raski and grabbed his ankle. Raski screamed. Zippy strapped a cowbell onto his ankle and broke its metal clasp so it would not open easily. She hopped up and proclaimed; "Now we can keep track of Raski wherever he goes!" Zippy hugged him like an anaconda squeezing its prey. All round the house the clanging of the bell could be heard as Raski ran around, chased by Zippy.

A few minutes later they all sat down at the kitchen table to eat breakfast.

"Welcome to Sloppy Breakfast. I'm your host, Joshi, and I don't like talking, but I have a talk show. This is the only talk show where people actually eat as they discuss issues that affect our daily lives, such as 'How far away can a dingo hear a cowbell' and 'Are there enough waffles to feed the entire studio audience?"

"I's hopes so," said Jÿger, passing a plate of French toast-flavored batteries to Fjordka.

"Sloppy Breakfast is good," said Lukkar, his mouth full of syrupy pancakes.

"Supposed what say me I am to show talk why not should?" said Emune as he bit into a cheese-filled danish with butter.

Joshi burped attempted to say something profound about boots and personality. People really do often leave their true selves outside with their shoes before going in to someone else's home. If people would keep their real selves with them all the time, there would be a lot less confusement, dirtier carpets, and more sloppy breakfast food to go around. Joshi couldn't explain what wearing shoes indoors had to do with breakfast food, but she figured what really mattered was that she did say something, even if it was irrational.

Life is like the
color blue.
No matter how
blue you know it
is, someone will
always insist it is
green.
What is blue?

Chapter 11

A severe case of mental constipation

Zippy sat on the sofa and unfolded the daily paper. Stocks were up, funds were down, lederhosen was in, kilts were out, and cabbage was smelly. Looking at the Funnies section provided far more insight into the world and its progress: Fluppy the puppy yawned and ate cat food by accident. Zippy turned to the sports section next. Woop! The Hjure Happynacks were headed to the shuffleboard final tournament. Last year, Wakezashi had front row seats to the Shuffleboard Bowl. The only news more intriguing than shuffleboard mania would be the want-ads.

Wanted: Computer Technician that can remove viruses and little siblings from computer / Wanted:

An instructor to teach formal kazoo lessons / Wanted: A double cheeseburger with fries; immediate; must be ready by noon / Wanted: silent doorbell / Wanted: Chef with experience handling Landenberg cheese, ask no questions / Missing: lucky ping—pong ball, yellow with . . .

. . . a criminal was apprehended under countless violations of jaywalking codes throughout the shady side of downtown, three blocks from the sunny side of downtown near the local watermelon orchard and apple vineyard.

The page stopped short at the spot where Zippy wanted to read on. Half of the page had been removed from the paper and she could see half of the next page under it, which featured an article on a fugitive jaywalker. "Hmmmn. Think, think, think again." She sighed and started again at the top of the want-ads page.

Wanted: Computer Technician that can remove viruses and little siblings from computer / Wanted: An instructor to teach formal kazoo lessons / Wanted: A double cheeseburger with fries; immediate; must be ready by noon / Wa

. . . And that was all there was! "Ehh! Fizzlewinks!" The page was shrinking . . . and the rest of the newspaper too, for that matter. She held up the front page. The paper felt really heavy. At the bottom were two teeth marks and a little rabbit hanging onto the paper with the clutches of its dear paws.

"Orange one of the Fungus! You ate the news! Well, you are what you eat." Orange Fungus chirped like a chorus of singing birds and climbed under the sofa. His footprints left text from the local stock report on the carpet.

In the meantime, Raski the Dingo Dude was 'running for his life' as he said, for the twelfth time that week. "The dingoes are coming coming coming coming! The dingoes dingoes dingoes are coming!" He ran down a dark alley, cowbell ringing, setting the first and last record speed for running from a dingo chase in an urban zone. He could see the shadows of dingoes . . . "I'll catch catch you dingo dingoes dingoes!" he muttered as he ran away from the overwhelming shadow of a fire hydrant. Raski was soon going so fast that he could not just stop running, so he fell into a skid of his rubber shoes on blacktop and veered right into a mailbox; the first chance he'd had to catch his breath.

Rainer walked outside and across the street to check the mail. Wind was northeast, clouds were cumulus, and Raski looked like he'd just fallen from the sky, like precipitation that melts in warm weather. "Good morning, Raski."

"So we meet again again again, my rival rival," said the panting boy using the wooden post as a leaning column. "This time time we shall shall shall shall see who will claim the the the title of of of of of of of ultimate pastry master!"

Rainer opened the mailbox and reached for the stack of mail. "Could you hand me that magazine?" he asked Raski.

"Oh, sure."

"Thank you."

"No problem—but but remember, only one one one among us can ever be worthy worthy worthy worthy of pastry master!"

Raski gave his opponent a good long stare before he started running again and crashed into the brick wall of Joshi's house. He straightened himself out and then rang the doorbell, which played a sound track of dogs barking viscously. Zippy came to the door and saw him panting like a puppy in the middle of a desert. Raski tried to say five things at once, but couldn't, so his tongue just waggled out of the corner of his mouth. He tried to run in three directions at once, straight forward so he could question Zippy about a suspicious dingo on the loose, to the right so he could capture the dingo he was after, and left to run away from the scary dingo that haunted his shadows. But he couldn't run in three directions at once, so his legs skittered and teetered like a child who has wet his pants for the very first time in public.

Zippy looked at the pathetic little boy standing four inches taller than she and saw something amusing in his face. She grabbed his cheek and stretched it away from his mouth. "Your cavity fortune says that if you fail to do what your dentist foretold, the toothache in your mouth will spread into your mind and consume your very being in acidic smog that emits an odor so strong it repels all dingoes for miles around." Zippy slowed down her words and patted him on the back. "What you need, my friend, is time." She strapped her watch onto his arm, and suddenly he felt ready to calmly walk inside and chat with her.

Joshi sat around pondering after breakfast. It was never safe to talk about a bad dream until after breakfast, or so her first-grade teacher had told her. Joshi once had a nightmare in which everyone was forced to wear pink all the time. Good thing she had eaten breakfast before she ever talked about it. Something like that would never happen in the Abyss. She wanted to visit the Abyss again so she could see all of the blueness surrounding her. Joshi went over to the kitchen window, but Emune wasn't there. She sat down at the window ledge and looked out at the forest in the backyard.

She could hear Raski squirming around on the living room floor complaining that Orange Fungus had 'ambushed' him by jumping out from under the couch when he sat down. After surprising him, the rabbit had crawled up his pants.

Zippy stood at the doorway. "Joshi, please come."

"Go where?"

"To the Abyss! Come, come see what has been done!" Zippy's eyes were as bright as fireworks.

Before she could blink, Joshi was falling down a toilet bowl head-first. She was soon covered in dark blue in all senses and directions, and although she felt Zippy's hand on her arm, she had no vision or way of hearing her. Words came into her head, but they had no voice attached to them.

> *The resentment about everything you ever knew . . .*

"You are not anyone I ever wanted to be, but still, you are me," Joshi whispered to her regrets.

> *You already had everything you've ever wanted before you even wished for it, and not in the Nevers, either. The truth here is not the truth of your life, but a possible truth. You wanted to be no one, so you were no one, until you became many someones. While one life and its world suffers, this one thrives. When this one falls, the other strives.*
>
> *You loved the original world. You played when you worked, and your playing was important work. You knew that, so even as your age began to leave immediate childhood, your soul remained, in order to do the work. It was that once you were given more rules, you learned time and lost the ability to do the work every day, for everything had its own jobs, and suddenly the world was not an endless place of an important duty, but a struggle.*
>
> *The saddest feeling you ever had was learning that you would always have to share the wonderful world with many people and give in to their ways, even if they mistreated the vibrant world. When you learned there was nowhere in that earth to avoid the influence of people, you had to choose between your*

fear of people on the wonderful earth or going to a place with no people and no earth. The brilliant earth could not be seen without facing the real people, and a world with no people had no real earth.

Despite the words swimming in Joshi's brain fluid, the world was still revolving.

Rainer and Raski opened up the pastry storage chamber. They knew it was against the rules to practice on official pastries beforehand, but each had caught the other in the act of doing so, and thus blackmailed one another. To their awe and horror, a loud burp echoed through the storage unit. The entire room was empty, except for a certain alien girl sitting in the corner and her furry companions. A small puppy and a bunny were licking jam off their faces, asleep in Zippy's lap. Their stomachs were so full they looked like bowling balls. "Contests aren't fun if you only care about winning!" said Zippy, and they all knew she was justified.

While Zippy was quite busy being in two places at once, in the pastry storage chamber and immersed in toilet travel, Joshi was trying to keep her focus in one place. Joshi read more words that wrote themselves into her mind:

You liked yourself because you were the only object you could predict and control, but then sadness split you into confusion where you now remain a soul in pieces. You learned to adapt and still keep your original soul, but it cost you your emotions.

As Ioshi you could make friends with boys that ignored girls. As Shorty, a five year-old, your siblings were obligated to take care of you because you enjoyed pretending to be so oblivious and naive to the world. As Psycho Luris, you were respected because you were tough and hit hard. You said it was okay to ignore others because you needed to do that in order to save yourself from them.

Joshi heard a voice, her own, from a memory she couldn't remember, a time when there was no time at all. She couldn't tell how old she had been when she said what she heard. "Just think of how much you like the earth, and trees. You can't live in a tree because there are things in trees: birds, lizards, squirrels, snipers. You can't live on the earth because there are things on the earth: librarians, cafeteria-workers, concrete, ladybugs, murderers, and people."

You said you could make up for things later, but never thought there would be a 'later' because Shorty still reminded you of your childishness, and you thought surely you'd die before adulthood because you never thought you could handle it. You gave yourself excuses to let others fear you, and after you changed personas again you wondered why even strangers continued to fear you, and it had been because they could see Psycho Luris dormant in you. You think you are an awful being, and assume all beings can see right

> *through you, so you're embarrassed around others. Animals like you because they can see right through you like you think, but humans cannot.*

Her voice started talking again and once more she did not remember the things she said, yet the feelings were familiar. "Come play in the dungeon. It's a little bit dark and damp, but there are no mean people there because there are no people there at all. Come play in the dungeon. The dungeon is fun in its own way, you'll see!"

Joshi's mind released some chaotic energy and relapsed into a memory of yesterday after she'd taught Lukkar a new trick. She got to try it out when Raski wanted to take her Hitherforme book.

"Please, Joshi, pleaseee let me borrow borrow your book book book for the dingo-trap fire! I promise it won't get too burnt, just singed to ashes ashes ashes."

"No."

Raski reached for the book anyway.

"Lukkar, pup-poo him!" And the result of what followed left Raski with and awful stain across his pants.

But Joshi's chaotic energy could not protect her forever, and there was more Joshi heard in her head. She had the confusion of a million memories all trying to be remembered at once:

> *There is a side of you that existed wonderfully once, and did so by ignoring the plight of her soul and thinking only of others. She is very strong and became*

so because she took interest in all aspects of the world, good and bad, and could assert herself to all. She was loved by people, but cried inside to herself because she was not born the person she wanted to be.

She was called Pokey, but she wanted to be called Yoshi. She would give anything to go to lands far away and waited a long time for a chance to leave, but no matter how many thousands of miles away she was, the same problems remained. She lived in the stories of the Yoshi Tokio she wanted to be.

Joshi had a headache and relapse into a dream. She saw a girl fighting Zippy as they crossed an ocean. Both of them looked to be the same age and about the same height. "Making enemies out of old friends is like using gold to make a toilet!" Zippy said. A battle map appeared in Joshi's mind, but faded when Joshi realized Zippy's opponent was Pokey. With everyone expecting Pokey to be perfect all the time and treating her as mighty, she created a foe that lived in her memories.

Joshi had not understood all that she was told, but she felt enlightened about something. Soon she and Zippy were visible again, and they continued down the toilet as if nothing had happened in the last five minutes. In fact, Joshi wasn't sure that there had even been a 'last five minutes' she could think of. As they fell they were entered a more physical place than the eye of the Abyss that Joshi had experienced. They landed in a familiar location, a bathroom covered in graffiti. Joshi heard voices and opened the door of the toilet stall.

Five girls in school uniforms, aged about second grade, sat on the floor playing poker. They sat on top of their cards when they noticed Zippy and Joshi were there.

"Please don't tell anyone. We're only playing a few rounds!"

"It's okay. We won't tell," reassured Zippy.

Zippy tilted open the door of a second stall. It opened up to a wide room covered in ice where some girls were playing hockey. She closed that door and opened yet another stall door, which was a very dark room. She pushed Joshi inside and closed the door behind them. Zippy flipped on the lights as confetti fell all around them. Qrsis and Fjordka yelled "Surprise!" as Zippy led Joshi to the center of the room where a table was with a platter of sausage with lighted candles sticking out of it.

"Happy Birthday, Joshi! We'll sing to you as you make a wish!" Their eyes were shining. Eyes . . . she was just thinking about something like that . . . the eye of the Abyss . . . or was it just a false memory? Eyes are in storms. Storms are battles. Battles are in people. A stormy battle called the Abyss was in the self of herself, and something that she didn't even purposely think about collided with her logic and yet forced the words together to make sense.

"But I don't think it's anytime near my birthday—it's not like I keep track of things like that very much, but I know it can't be very near."

"Silly Joshi," said Fjordka, "Today is your birthday on Mercury! Now start blowing out the candles or your piece of Polish bratwurst will be covered in wax!"

I wish this friendly moment would last forever, even in battle, even in reality, even when I am no one again.

It was an exciting party for the four girls. They played pin-the-nose-on-the-elephant, joke-or-dare, and squirt-the-weird-one, a game in which they did rock-paper-scissors and whoever had a different sign than the rest was squirted with paint. By the end of the party they all had paint all over themselves. Blue paint hung on Joshi's hair and orange paint striped Fjordka's face and arms. "Till next time!" said Joshi. Qrsis hugged her and Joshi hugged back. She had forgotten what it felt like to hug something other than a stuffed animal.

Back in another dimension, the boys' bathroom, Raski casually walked in and took his time, in pace with the steady jingle of the cowbell on his shoe. He was planning on looking for dingoes in the next half hour and after that he'd decided he would spend an hour running from the dingoes. Raski relaxed and finished his business. He looked at his watch, but it didn't hold still long enough for it to tell the time, for it had begun to wiggle. The watch unclasped from around his arm and fell to the floor, where it spontaneously combusted. Alarmed, Raski jumped in midair and had just pulled up his pants when he started to gallop away, for there was never enough time to catch the dingoes, no sir!

Zippy and Joshi were walking back to the house when Raski ran past them on the street. He was followed by not dingoes, but by a few police officers yelling something about jaywalking. Raski didn't seem to notice them, though, because he was muttering about dingoes again.

"He's going so fast, when will he notice his fly's unzipped?"

"I dunno . . . HEY RASKI, LOOK DOWN AND ZIP UP!"

Chapter 12

Welcome to Knighthood, Sir Joshi

"Zippy, where's Emune?"

"He was growing very quickly for such a little plant, so in the backyard did I plant him."

Joshi searched the forest in the lot situated behind her apartment. So many trees . . . there's a blue tree? No, it was . . . something foreign with leafy stalks, planted in a pebble bed. Something called Emune, it was. Emune was asleep, unable to come into human form. Looking at a sleeping bamboo plant made Joshi tired.

She discovered a snail inching down the main stalk of Emune and decided to follow it. Walking beside it, Joshi's shadow was cast over the snail, protecting it from the sunny heat. While Joshi slowly followed it, she took careful steps as to not walk over the path the snail left behind it, for it was like a record of the snail's journeys. The snail made its way to the sidewalk, the freeway of snail travel. When suddenly . . . danger alert! Bicycler, at three 'o clock, southbound, on a rampage from the last exit.

The snail wiggled its antennae to the right, a turn signal, but the biker didn't see. Two thundering deadly wheels came closer and closer . . . Joshi reached over and picked up the snail just before the biker whipped by. She took a good look at the bicycle as it sped away. "No license plate, reckless habitual driving, that is." She turned back to the snail, making sure it was uninjured. "You remind me of someone I used to know."

Joshi started to scout out a place in the grass to put down the snail a few feet from the threats of the sidewalk. She had just put down the snail when she began to feel very oddly different. She wasn't changing, but everything outside of her was. The violet grass hadn't been violet before, and she'd remembered a hazel sky, not an orange one. The clouds puffed together underneath the outlines of trees and formed the shapes of snails and squirrels.

Lukkar, who had been riding in Joshi's jacket hood, barked and twitched his now-blue fur towards the increasingly robust wind. He jumped down to the grass near the sidewalk and left a blurry multicolor shadow in the wind. His smoky fur glowed fluorescently from the moment his paws touched the ground. A knife blade shot up through a crack in the pavement. Hitherforme pushed back the two pieces of sidewalk in blocks and squeezed through.

"Compassion for the small," said Hitherforme, "is a virtue that makes you worthy of knighthood." Hitherforme sheathed her dagger and drew out a hockey stick from the back of her belt.

"Kneel if you accept this position."

"What's the job description?"

"Just kneel. You don't really have a choice in this—defenders of the snails are bestowed honors and favors they cannot avoid."

Joshi imagined wearing a clunky suit of armor twice her weight and commanding a steed that probably had dreams of winning the Kentucky Derby instead of transporting soldiers to jousting competitions. "But I want to be a ninja. This must be some kind of mistake. And please don't give me a horse. All I wanted last Christmas were some shuriken throwing stars."

"Don't worry. We don't have the budget for horses . . . or shurikens for that matter. But you really must kneel now."

Despite her misgivings Joshi knelt anyway. She couldn't help but admit to herself she felt pretty brave and tough that her rescue had drawn the attention of Hitherforme. "So, what exactly is being a knight all about?"

Hitherforme popped her knuckles and yawned. "I wouldn't rightly know. I'm a supa' hiiiroo, not a medieval minion—no offense to the position—I'm just like a magical cop—donut breaks, working paycheck and everything." She waved around the hockey stick and touched Joshi's shoulder with the blade.

"Kewl! What's that do? Does it have some magical properties or an attack advantage?"

Hitherforme wondered if *kewl* was any different from *cool*. "No, it's just a regular old hockey stick, got it on sale for a good price, a lot cheaper than the katana I thought about getting for you—no offense—but, y'know, my supa'hiiroo costume costs a fortune to dry clean." Hitherforme cleared her throat and projected her voice. "A'hem, you are knighted 'Sir Joshi', tomboy ninja of the mystical hockey stick, and you, Lukkar, are the one and only official 'sidekick' of the ninja, complete with the ability to communicate with Joshi!"

"Uh, he already knew how to do that."

Hitherforme shrugged. "Yeah, I know, but I had to say something to make it sound special."

"Special is good," said Lukkar.

"Here are the details of your quest-mission-thingy," instructed Hitherforme. She handed Joshi a restaurant menu. "There you will receive the details of your mission from a very talented karaoke lip-sinker. You may appoint a squire at any time, but choose carefully, 'cause there's only one, and if they quit there's no picking new ones, and good luck. Oh, and I recommend you try the shrimp-flavored ramen served on a stick; very appetizing, that place." With another wave Hitherforme left Joshi. Joshi held her hockey stick over one shoulder with the blade pointed behind her like a weapon of the grim reaper.

"One place to go, Luk. Hope you like udon as much as I do!"

"Udon is good."

"You got that right!"

Half an hour later, Joshi stepped inside the building with a huge "HAPPY RAMEN" sign outside it. Immediately a smell she'd missed filled her mind, probably reaching it through her ears, because her nose was stuffy. The smell was like fresh goulash cooking over a fire (or a grill or stove). Joshi didn't exactly know what goulash was, but in a way she thought of the dish as a European ramen equivalent. Anything with her two favorite food groups, meat and noodles, could not be turned down. What other food groups could there possibly be, anyway?

The shop walls were as flavorful as the smells of fresh ramen. They were covered in amusing signs that said things like "Welcome to Happy Ramen, the ramen shop of smiles! Sit down and chow down while you occur happy thoughts. We like our customers to feel happy, happy, happy."

Joshi felt comfortable bringing her hockey stick in with her because from looking at the place it seemed to be a casual lunch spot for people with unusual interests. A TV in the corner was tuned in to a table tennis match, a four-team foosball table was across from the bar-style seats, and on a small platform were a karaoke machine and a broken microphone stand with an old flashlight taped to the top where a microphone should have been.

Going up to the counter, Joshi saw a waitress in a polka-dotted apron tied with curly ribbons. "You must be Joshi."

"How'd you . . ?"

"We know all of our regulars here because that's all the customers we get. Please wait here and feel free to look over our happy menu while I fetch the one you seek. Here also is a happy canine menu for your puppy."

Strange, but nice, thought Joshi. *Most of the time it's not like that. Usually, my name is like a crater on Mars. Everyone's heard of it, but no one knows what it is.*

A moment later, none other than Zippy herself came out of the back room, in the same uniform as the waitress.

"The star karaoke lip-sinker is here!"

"Somehow I should've known . . ."

"Sit down and we shall eat while we talk, I mean, talk in between eating, or eating in between talking."

Joshi ordered beef-flavored udon in a cup, and Zippy ordered tofu-flavored ramen in a taco shell with extra soy sauce. There were many choices on the menu, which included over ten flavors of ramen and the many ways it could be served: in a bowl, on a plate, on a kabob stick, on a pizza crust, in an ice cream cone, and in a hamburger bun, just to name a few.

Zippy pulled out an envelope from under her apron. Joshi recognized it as the letter she'd written to Zippy many days ago. "I just received this today because it was delivered by a snail. I shall read it now."

Dear Zippy,
I would really like to know what your objectives are in taking me to this place. I want to know

"Barf in a . . . uh, beef in a cup and also, um, soy with extra soy in taco, your orders up!" announced the clerk-boy at the counter, interrupting the reading of the letter.

"Thanks to you and have happy time with happy food," greeted the smiling waitress as they went up to the counter to get their food.

They sat down again, and Zippy started over.

Dear Zippy,
I would really like to know what your objectives are in taking me to this place. I want to know why it matters that I am here, and I don't know which person I am.

"Umm, Zippy, you seem a bit irritated by something. Do you have allergies?" Again the letter was interrupted.

"No, the situation is, I have combat pants on rolled up underneath my skirt, and it isn't the most comfortable feeling. Gotta be prepared at all times for unexpected ninja missions."

"Oh. Anyway, continue."

> *and I don't know which person I am. I feel like I could easily be either Yoshi or Joshi in real life, and it's almost like I don't know which life to return to. I feel like noise putty that been stretched into many globs of goo that seem similar but are in many different places. I don't know which memories are real and which are fake. It's like I've tried to mimic a story with my life and succeeded so much that I don't know what place I'm in anymore or if I'm supposed to be there. I don't want to be exploited. By the way, I miss eating udon and I want to know if Hitoshi's doing alright.*
>
> *Sincerely but not sincere,*
> *Joshi*

"Joshi, that's so sweet to write a letter. How nice to show concern for your old friends."

"Friends?"

"You stated concern for Hitoshi and you showed appreciation for me by writing it to me. You could've written a letter to the president of the United States, but you chose to write a letter to me!"

"Do you think you can explain what I asked about in the letter?"

"I can't answer your questions."

"Aww, man, why?"

"Because you've already answered them. First of all, after writing the letter you found out where you were, that is, in the World of Nevers. Second of all, it wasn't me who brought you here; it was you. Third of all, you want to know which person you are originally, and that would be the person you were before any data changes. Forth of all, only you can put yourself in a place, so you need to go to different places to collect all pieces of your memory. Fifth of all, I can't make Hitoshi appear out of nowhere because this ain't no sappy fairy tale where I could just zap Lukkar so he'd turn into Hitoshi. Hitoshi's doing fine, and you need to focus most on yourself, no matter how many people you are. Sixth of all, well, I don't have a sixth point, but seventh of all, are you going to eat all of that?" She pointed to the udon beef bowl.

"What's my first ninja mission, Zippy?"

"Both you and I have already stated it. You must prepare to go wherever you must in order to find all pieces of yourself so you can decide which life you have and which you do not, and where you are really standing on the earth. You are weary from confusion and many lifetimes of chaos that twist your brain and drain your fluids." Zippy took a piece of tofu in her hand and rolled it together like a ball of noise putty. "I suggest you hibernate before the noon of this summer, so you'll be asleep during the sticky hot weather you despise. When you hibernate for a month or so, you will sleep, really sleep, without interrupted confusion and chaos, but with a peaceful clarity that will give you strength. I suggest Lukkar go with you into hibernation, because you don't have a stuffed animal you can take with."

Joshi left the ramen shop to find a suitable place to hibernate. It would need to be near food and in an enclosed soft place. The eye of the Abyss would do it, a place all blue. Joshi ran to the Abyss with a new strength in her kinetic link to the earth, as fast as a wolf, but with the willpower of a snail.

"How do you like knighthood, Sir Joshi?" asked Emune.

"I dunno. It's not as weird as berserking. How do you like being outside all the time? Anyway, Lukkar and I are going to the Abyss, and I'm taking five pounds of udon with me for hibernation preparation."

Up in a tree many feet away from Emune, a snail was watching, winking its eyes the way snails do when they're happy because they are incapable of smiling.

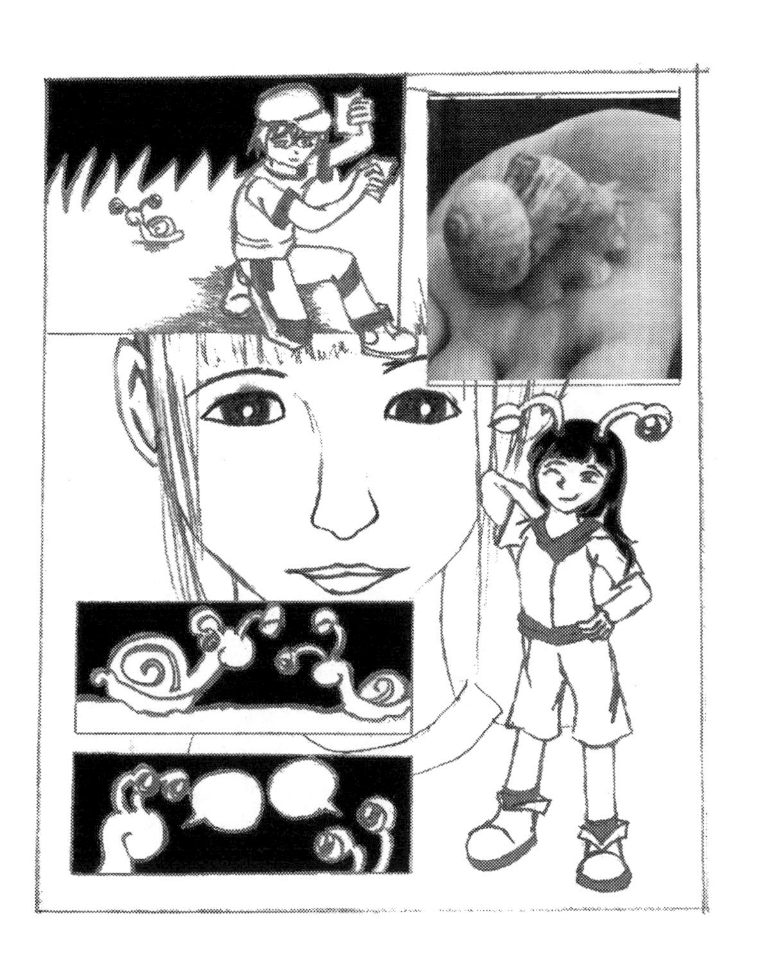

Chapter 13

A dragon named Snarg

Joshi woke up in a pool of her own drool from hibernating the past month. Lukkar was still asleep nearby, and as he slept his tail swished back and forth on the padded floor, and he whispered things like "Blue is good." Joshi crawled across the bumpy surface molded with the texture of rock-shaped pillows. She thought she saw something yellow drifting in the blue mist, but it faded away into aqua before another second passed. She'd never seen such a color in the Abyss before. At the opposite wall of the fragile chamber, Joshi pushed back layers of soft pillowy bricks till she reached in and felt no more softness, but air. Pulling back a long drape of fuzzy blue mist-colored material, she found a window about the size of herself.

The window let in every color of the light spectrum and more. Some colors she'd never seen before, not even a close hue or intensity like them. The new colors cannot be described in words; it is very difficult to describe a color such as red because in different variations it can hold different properties familiar to all colors, such as intensity, shade, and light. Therefore the only way to give even a vague description of a color to one who has never seen it is to describe not the color, but its effects on one's self, such as blue is said to generate a feeling of sadness.

However, even this system of color identification is very haphazard; what one sees that may make one happy could make another sad. It has been proven already (and inadvertently) that it would be difficult and next to impossible for you to understand the colors by how they affected Joshi or anyone else, because when Joshi is surrounded by blue she is the most exuberantly pleased. Thus, blue, certainly does not make everyone sad. It may be because it is the color of water, and water makes up tears, and tears often represent sadness and despair, that blue is associated with sorrow. Nonetheless, water is not always cold like ice, nor always in the form of tears, and tears are not always out of sadness either.

Regardless of faulty conclusions, you will hear with your mind (I call it reading) about the effects of the new colors on Joshi's mind. Like any artist, having seen past normal human limits, Joshi immediately wanted to pick up a paintbrush and capture the never before seen colors in paint. But the colors were like warped wind, making it hard even to see them long enough to keep a memory of it. There was a color for wisdom, a color for patience, and a color for insanity. One color said 'fight,' another said 'sleep.'

A small shade of blue mixed with one of the colors, but Joshi couldn't describe what the color was like, only that it was part blue and part something she'd never seen before. Joshi had never seen anything so colorful in her life as this alien world she saw now looking out the window. The most colorful thing she'd ever seen before had been multicolored raccoon feces she'd found in a swamp, and now it hardly could compare.

Lukkar woke up and jumped onto her shoulders. Joshi had been so fascinated by the strange place outside that she hadn't noticed his waking and was startled by his jump. She was losing her balance,

and

falling

farther

and farther

away from the

blue she did not want to

forget, what was . . . what?

What was blue. The sky is blue (when it is not orange, that is).

"I feel like I've been everywhere in the boundaries of the Nevers. That's why I need some sky," said Hitherforme. "A piece of sky would be good for building a watchtower, so I could look beyond miles and see if there's any small spot in this world I've never seen. It would also help Jÿger, whose little cousin is always getting lost."

"It would help help help me, too too," said the only word-echoing dingo dude around. "I I I could watch for for those tricky tricky tricky dingo dingoes."

"Let's get started building it, then."

"But but but we still need a piece piece piece piece of something light and floaty floaty for high-up views, like a piece of sky sky sky."

"I'll throw a boomerang way up high that'll scrape off a bit of sky for us to use."

"But But what if if you hit a a a a a bird or or an air-o-plane or or a flying dingo?"

"Hmm, true. Hadn't thought of that."

"I I I know where where Wakezashi is is is keeping a piece piece of sky we can can can steal."

"Blarg, you Rask-al. I'm a supa' hiirroo. I ain't steal'n. But I'll handcuff you if you do, ya dingo!"

"Yes yes, ma'am."

"Let's go see Wakezashi."

Joshi felt very dizzy. She was laying in some sort of ditch with Zippy sitting next to her, shaking her shoulders. "Joshi wake up, wake up NOW! Joshi, oh please Joshi! If you don't wake up and say you're alive, I'll hate you forever!"

"I'm . . . okay, I guess. I just remember falling from a window."

"Joshi, I don't know how you could have gotten here—this place isn't connected to the plumbing route. When you fell, your landing impact created this thirty foot crater. I'm really glad you're not hurt." Zippy hugged her. "Joshi, look around. This planet is my home. This place is called Kazzorran."

Jÿger got up from his stool by the fireplace when he heard the knock on the door. He hoped it was good news. A little boy sat on top of a floating dragon the size of a microwave.

Jÿger picked up his little cousin and hugged him. "Imp, goods to sees you, buddy!" The dragon followed them inside and Jÿger fed it some toast and crackers. He patted its head. "Thank you, Snarg. It's hard to keep track of Imp when I'm working so many jobs. Please tell your master I am very grateful."

"Broda! (Brohhdaa)" squealed three year-old Imp, as if Jÿger were his own brother. Imp pulled a corn dog out of his pocket and chewed on it before stuffing it through Snarg's nostrils. The dragon decided it was time to fly off again to its master Hitherforme.

A flash of light put Joshi in a trance and soon Joshi was in the bathroom-turned-swamp in the World of Nevers. To Joshi Zippy's home planet was like a memory of a dream. Apparently someone had been expecting Joshi's return to the World of Nevers, for above the commode was sign that read: *Welcome Home, Joshi!*

"Yo, Joshi!" yelled Zippy from the kitchen, "Come see—I've found something I never knew was here before!"

Joshi rushed over to where Zippy was by the window.

"Look under the windowsill, there's a button there."

"What'll happen if we press it?"

"I dunno. Let's find out!"

Someone should have explained to them that finding random buttons in odd places is dangerous and usually signifies something that ought not to be screwed up. One such example is how Zippy and Yoshi messed up this story by clicking a button on the author's computer that they should have never found. But alas no one was there with Zippy and Joshi to warn them about the hazard of pressing random buttons. After pressing the button on under the windowsill both Zippy and Joshi were in a place neither of them had ever been before (and hopefully neither of them will ever end up there again). They were standing in the dimension of the author of this story.

"Hey, you, typing at the computer!" greeted Zippy, "What's up with all of this?"

"You tell me. Here's your scripted predicted reply right here."

"Hmm, that's not very exciting."

"What do you mean it's not very exciting!!!!???!????!?!?!??"

"Never mind." Zippy reverted back to canine form and wagged her tail.

"Excuse me," said Joshi, "why bother writing this story?"

"Because I feel it is important to me, and to the sake of explaining insanity."

"I know you just said sake, but because it was typed and not spoken out loud for other readers, we won't really know if you meant 'sake' as in an English idiomic noun or 'sake,' referring to the Japanese alcoholic beverage." said Zippedity. The author started typing out the longer form of Zippy's name, now that she was being obnoxious.

"Do I look like a bartender to you?"

Zippy stuck her tongue out at the author. "Actually, you . . ."

"Vil de vaere sa venlig . . . a st osto preadin gto ofa rahea di nth escript?!" Shouted the author, half in Danish, half in thick Kentucky accent which pulled letters from the words before the last in a not-so-unusual pattern, slightly familiar to anyone who'd ever heard Jÿger speak.

"Umm, she's done more than just that already . . ." said Joshi, pointing to the computer screen, where Zippedity Zhong had typed her own 'edits' into the story (what I call randomly deleting sentences and pounding on the keyboard till it beeps like a bleeped out cuss word on TV).

HIUDHIWHWHiuhhyyhue0it4iyoyoyoyoyoyjeitjo uujuhyr83y92y 'dxjwieueuruerpewrp[wr ^^★%&(★@—=0=33kjgpopiuguwe[0ti-34)IEIJD(JW\\=\\\\\\ 45664kopit3t ÿÿÿ1:??ÆÅÄô1+

"That's enough, Zipedity!"

Zippy withdrew from the keyboard, but not without getting in one last htoihwrto;re;eqhtr;hqeroiqhreottqoreht ohrtoho pound of squiggle marks across the page to prove she'd been there.

"I should be paid for being such a great character!" said Zippedity.

"I hope I don't have to pay you to get you to leave!"

"Hej, um, author-person," said Joshi, "why do you have to make me such an introverted character? Why can't I hold everyone's attention better, like Zippy, who has lots of fans?"

"Because I'm that way, too. Bye, Zippy!"

"But I'm not leaving just yet!" said the multicolored dog named Zippedity.

"That was your cue to go!"

Zippedity stuck her tongue out again. "You're much crueler to your characters than other authors!"

"Why? Because I let kids act like kids, dogs act like people, and bunnies act like dingoes? Sue me!"

"I will."

"That's great, especially since you're my lawyer." Zippedity folded her arms in a matter-of-fact manner.

"I am?"

"Yeah, and you agreed to it. Just ask Joshi." Zippedity stuck out her tongue a third time.

Joshi finally spoke again. "Somehow, I've been having this feeling for a long time, and it feels a lot like I've never left chapter four."

"Buy a copy of the text and look at that chapter, and maybe you'll figure it out." The author looked around uneasily. "By the way, if you hadn't seen your paintbrush lately, it's because I've been using it for my self portrait painting." The author gave the Joshi runic paintbrush back to Joshi.

A few minutes later and Zippy and Joshi were out of the author's sight and safely down the toilet to their own little story bubble.

HUDHWHh7h6iuriewhtweeutoiuw]uroepwiutorut rotiopektoewk e[pop6o

Too bad the author wasn't able to catch all of the editing marks Zippedity made earlier, because obviously what the author had thought to be the last of Zippy's edits was not.

"See that, Snarg?" said Hitherfome, "That piece of sky looks opaque when it's floating above the base now, but as soon as it gets farther up in the air, it will look transparent, and when you're standing on the tower elevator it will seem as if you're floating!" Snarg wasn't too excited; she'd already seen the secrets of the skies. Being born with wings leaves you with less imagination. Snarg looked up at Hitherforme.

"Do you have something you want to say, Snarg?"

"Snarg," said Snarg.

Jÿger finished his paperwork and flexed his knuckles. He felt something in his pocket and pulled out a corn dog. Then he looked around the room. Imp was missing, again.

Raski was running around with the cowbell tied to his ankle ringing. He saw a little kid with a yellow dot sticker on his forehead approach him. The kid was eating a corn dog, and his pockets were stuffed full of them.

"Hi, little little kid. Can I have have a corn dog dog?"

"No!"

Raski bent down to the kid's eye level. "Please, please. I only only only want one." Imp kicked Raski in the crouch, which made him back away. "Okay, okay, you win win win."

From above in the sky Snarg saw Imp's tantrum and flew down to him. "That's the dingo dude Raski," said Snarg.

Imp pointed at Raski. "Diggo!"

Raski ran off.

Soon Snarg, Hitherforme and Imp met up with Zippy and Joshi, and they all went up on the piece of sky to the observation tower.

Snarg was whispering into Imp's ear. "All you see around you is only the surface of this world. Even though you think you see it all, there is always undiscovered territory above the clouds or below the ground."

"Not so!" said Imp

"Yes so!" said Snarg, "It is the indefinite truth, after all."

"Diggo!" squealed Imp, jumping up and down at the sight of Diggo running past the watch tower on the ground below. Diggo's cowbell was still strapped to him and still ringing. A Raski chased Diggo on the ground and then four more Raskis also ran by in a pack. From the watch tower they look as small as snails. Imp clapped his hands, shaking loose a corn dog from his pocket.

A few blocks away, Jÿger was searching for Imp when he saw a corn dog falling from the sky. He caught it and wondered if he was in his right mind. Raski offered to pay him fifty dollars for the corndog, and then Jÿger really began to question if he was actually awake.

Meanwhile, Hitherforme looked out across the expansive miles of land she'd known for so long. There was one place she'd never been before. Just one. She looked a thin glowing line that stretched in all directions around the edge of the town. "What is that?" she asked Joshi.

"It's called the horizon line." said Joshi. "No matter where you are in the air or the up in the tower here there will always be one, a point that you cannot see past."

"I want to cross this horizon," said Hitherforme, stunned by the view.

Hitherforme was not the only one surprised. Joshi hadn't ever considered that others might not know all the same things she did.

"It is impossible to go beyond all horizons, though." said Zippy, "Because no matter where you are there one will still be waiting to be crossed in all directions.

"It is the indefinite truth, after all," said Hitherforme, her head literally and figuratively in the clouds.

Chapter 14

Joshi in Wonderland

"If everything disappeared tomorrow, what color would the universe be?" Joshi asked.

"Universe is good" was the only response she received from anyone listening.

"Is a black hole a spot where a dimension has been erased?" Joshi scratched her head. "I believe that the colors of human eyesight may be relative to the viewer. What I see as blue might be what you see as gray, but know as blue. Therefore, every animal has a chance to see blue. We should accept that what is blue to me is violet to Zippy, or yellow to Jÿger. Yellow is Jÿger's blue, and no one should take that away from him." She scratched her head again. "If what I believe is different than those of others, but just as important to the earth, then don't I have the right to maintain my own thoughts?" Joshi stroked Lukkar's ears. "Is any of this making sense to you?" Lukkar blinked.

"I have a new theory," Joshi continued, "that not only is the earth and the principles of its dimensions relative to the one seeking answers, but people are also relative to the seeker. I don't think any two people will ever describe a particular scene in exactly the same way, nor will any two people think of someone with the exact same thoughts. If the world is what we make it out to be, why aren't people what we make them out to be? It is because people know the nature of their own kind, but people do not know the truth of the earth because they do not remember being a part of it, as they do remember their occurring human lives."

Emune was running through the forest, blue in the face and gasping for air. Wakezashi, who had been picking mushrooms in a yard close by, dropped everything and ran to Emune when she saw him. He collapsed in her arms like a wilted vine of ivy. "Say something, Emune. Speak to Wakezashi and say that you're alright." He looked like he was trying to talk, but the best he could do was spit out some drainage from his throat. "Wakezashi will take Emune to water." With that, the short girl lifted up Emune, a much taller and heavier being, and heaved him across her shoulders.

Zippy sat on a tree branch, spying on Jÿger as he made door-to-door deliveries dragging his messenger bag behind him with Imp in it. "Row, row, row your boat gently down the stream! Merrily, merrily, merrily, merrily, life is but a neverending world—domination scheme!" Zippy sang as she watched Imp sneak a corn dog into the address-label pouch of a package. Jÿger wiped the sweat from his forehead. Joshi kept singing. "How much is that puppy in the window? The one with fuzzy blue fur?" Then Wakezashi came into view. She carried something. Zippy hoped it wasn't some sort of science experiment. Then Wakezashi came closer and Zippy noticed it looked like a person. This could be serious! She was on the run in a flash.

Emune lay on a bed of rocks and water that Wakezashi prepared. The rocks and water were very much relieving to his pains, for they were the substance that gave him life from the pebbled soil he rooted in.

"What is the ailment?" asked Zippy.

"Kudzu." Wakezashi held up Rune's right hand. His fingernails were looking green, and some green plant stuff was creeping out of them.

"We must fight the kudzu!"

"Fighting it will be useless unless you find the source."

"I shall prepare my troops for battle!" And that Zippy did.

Five minutes later, Zippy and her 'troops,' Joshi, Lukkar, and Snarg (Hitherforme hadn't been found soon enough to recruit her), ventured out into the forest to find where Emune had been.

"When in doubt, look up," said Zippy. They stood in the wake of a giant blue bamboo stalk two feet in diameter that reached all the way into the sky, with a snot-green vine twisting around it.

"To find the source . . ." Zippy began.

"Follow the path to it." Joshi completed.

Zippy reverted to her canine form in order to climb the stalk more easily, and Joshi stuck her hockey stick between the back of her shirt and her jacket. Lukkar and Zippy led the way climbing up, and Snarg was already far ahead because she could just fly to the top. The whole stalk shook from the suctioning force of the kudzu's control. Joshi climbed up by holding on to bamboo limbs, and the dogs went up by digging their claws into the snot-green kudzu that wrapped around the blue bamboo shoots.

Jÿger had made his last delivery and was heading home when Orange Fungus jumped unexpectedly out of his messenger bag. "Fuzzy-Wuzzy Squirrel!" squealed Imp. Jÿger sighed. No wonder his messenger bag had seemed extra heavy today. "Nots squirrel," he coached Imp, "Rabbit."

"Not so!"

"Is so's, Imp."

"Na-uh."

Jÿger walked further along the sidewalk until he saw a large hole in the pavement that looked as if it had been cut open. Imp leaned over the bag to take a look, but leaned too far, sending the whole messenger bag with him in it down the hole, followed by Jÿger who held onto the bag for dear life. They landed on a soft turf that crunched under their weight.

Orange Fungus sniffed the air and bounded down a cave-like tunnel behind Imp and Jÿger. They followed him. The floor was sticky, covered in glops of a honey-brown clay. It did not occur to Jÿger until he saw a stream of the liquidified clay that it was peanut butter, and very delicious! After lots of sampling, he looked all around the peanut butter aqueduct he'd discovered. Jÿger could be rich if he mined the place! He could make lots of money if he jarred the peanut butter and sold it. Peanut butter could also be useful as fuel for airplane engines and produce energy for factory machines and scrumptious electricity. He had discovered the jackpot of jackpots—natural resources and food to last a lifetime, and a rich luxurious lifetime that would be!

Suddenly the sound of scampering foxes and squirrels filled the echoes of the cavern. One by one a small fuzzy animal appeared to take a drink of peanut butter, and then in larger and larger groups. Some animals seemed desperate for the peanut butter, and others looked as healthy and as casual as if they came to the aqueduct for daily meals. Jÿger rethought his future. If he mined the peanut butter, the aqueduct would no longer be able to replenish itself with peanut butter for the animals to eat and drink. By taking it away it could all be used up faster than intended. Peanut butter was valuable, like money, but even more valuable was the health of the world.

Joshi, Zippy, Lukkar, and Snarg continued going upwards until they finally reached a small stretch of land at the top where stood a library covered in kudzu. Snarg had just landed and was walking along when she tripped on a root coming out of the kudzu-covered ground. A net of kudzu sprung over her and trapped her in its vines. Lukkar ran to help her but got stuck himself. Zippy went back into human form to untangle them, but the kudzu quickly enveloped her too in a large knot with the rest.

"Joshi, stay back! You must find the source and destroy it, or we'll have no hope of getting out!"

Joshi tiptoed cautiously around the kudzu and up to the front door of the library. Two gatekeeper librarians guarded the entrance.

"Halt! Who goes there?"

"I would like access to the library in order to check out a book, please." Joshi sensed an evil wit around the librarians; they seemed to like the kudzu.

"No non-librarians are permitted on this premises. How dare you not bow before the head-librarian!"

Joshi made a short bow, and the head librarian snorted. "Only librarians are worthy of these books! Trespassers are ensnared in our pet kudzu."

Joshi tried a different route. "Miss, perhaps I haven't told you, I should very much like to be a librarian when I grow up and would very much like to be trained in the ways of the kudzu library."

The head librarian wasn't so sure about Joshi's excuse, but the other one bought Joshi's story like a bargain shopper at a used book store.

"Perhaps, if you answer my riddle I will not feed you to the kudzu and permit you entry."

"Okay! Um, I mean, yes miss!"

"What is it that can be good or evil, smart or dumb, kind or wicked, helpful or discourteous, and can hoard knowledge to keep it away from all other animals?"

It was only too easy. "A human!"

"Wrong answer! If you wanted to be a librarian, you would know that the answer was 'a librarian'!"

"But a career is not the same as a species, as indicated when you said 'all other animals!'"

"That's where you are wrong. We evil librarians have developed into a new sub-human species in order to fight those traitor kind librarians that actually let dumb children learn and touch the pages of books with their grubby little paws! We evil librarians are powerful and our objective is not to let others enjoy reading and knowledge, but to ensure that only us are the ones who know anything worth knowing!" ⋆Cackle⋆

Joshi drew out her hockey stick and said a heroic line as if she were a character in one of the action-genre mangas she enjoyed. "Well, there's one thing worth knowing that you don't know, and that's that book knowledge is useless against the will of the truth of good and evil!" ⋆SMACK⋆ went Joshi's hockey stick in the crotch of the librarian (didn't faze the librarian) . . . ⋆SMACK⋆ broke the glass window of the door and shot through in a ninjutsu blast. Joshi knocked out the librarians with a pile of heavy books that had been sitting on the window sill.

Once inside, Joshi covered the broken door in tape from the check-out desk. The inside of the building was covered in kudzu also, and the chains of kudzu connected to the spine of each book. She didn't see any huge piles of knotted kudzu like she'd expected, so she figured the source must be inside a book.

Joshi's first plan of action was to run to the card catalog and look up any books with "kudzu" or "evil librarian" in the title, but Joshi wasn't very good with numbers and the kudzu draped everywhere hid a lot of signs and numbers on the shelves which may have otherwise been useful. She wandered over to a shelf and picked up a particularly large book. She may as well start somewhere. Joshi tried opening the book to the center pages in order to see if the vine connected to it was the source of the kudzu, but the book would not open to any page except for page 1. After she'd read the first page, she was able to turn to the next one, page by page of reading.

To her surprise, She began to really like the book. It was titled *The Ever-Incomplete Book of Nonsense.* The book's format looked like a volume of an encyclopedia, but clearly it was written to be read page by page instead of used for alphabetical or numerical reference. Nonetheless, at the top of every page was a guide indicating what the last page had on it and what the current page did and the first entry of the next page. The only way for anyone to really even begin to understand what sort of book Joshi was reading is to read an excerpt yourself:

> *~Bangladesh~ ~racketball~ page 4 ~tofu salad~*
>
> *was speaking* ***Bengali****, but is now playing* ***racketball****. Speaking of* ***racketball****,* ***racketball*** *is next in the disorder of vocabulary and entries in this non-textbook text.* ***Racketball*** *is a board game consisting of shoots, ladders, cheese sandwiches, and a sleepy scorekeeper.* ***Racketball*** *consists of making the most racket ever imagined while bouncing a bouncy ball on top of the board game board while wiggling your middle toe clockwise, your pinky finger counter-clockwise, and keeping your nose perfectly still.* ***Racketball*** *is illegal in thirteen countries worldwide and is partially responsible for the spelling of the other racket-and-ball sport to be "raquetball", quite to the dismay of the National System of Federal Numerics Society, which claims one number must be placed in each word for it to be spelled correctly but not written, given that at the time the words are not written but spoken and later written, later being within twenty to ninety days later when a credit card bill is paid, they are written while sitting, and not standing, in line to order food at a* ***Bengali*** *fast food place with* ***tofu salads*** *on the menu. Speaking of* ***tofu salad****,* ***tofu salad*** *is next in the disorder of vocabulary and entries in this non-textbook text.*

When Joshi finally got to the middle of the nonsensical book and saw that the kudzu in the middle was not the source, she looked at the spines of many other books, including a diary she picked up that was written in runic. Like an instinct she pulled her paintbrush of her shoes and held it up to the pages. It glowed blue and transformed the text in the diary from computer font type to handwritten letters. The entries she read were very sad, and to her disappointment, offered no clue as to where the source of the kudzu could be. A large "K" was engraved on the cover of the diary, but she would never know if it was meant to be the Western alphabet letter 'K' or the Danish runic symbol, 'K' which in Danish runic script was used as the letter 'P.'

The diary mentioned an angel, and the description of the angel was very curiously like the guardian angel Joshi had dreamed of when she was hibernating. She had not thought about her hibernation since the day she woke up from it. Joshi knew there were such things as angels, but she had not known before that other people were capable of seeing the same visions she had. There before her was proof that her visions, previously undisclosed to anyone else, not even the author of this book, had been real.

So people know the truth, but do not always admit the extent of their knowledge, for it may coincide with another's beliefs, or with their own personal goals.

Joshi noticed an illustration on its back cover, a sketch of the angel described in the book, a boy that looked exactly like herself, like Ioshi but with wings. Joshi felt scared for

Ioshi, her friend and animus. If he were an angel, would he would ever return to his rightful place? She didn't mind being Ioshi, but she knew that some feelings are too heavenly for earth. Joshi wanted to protect Ioshi from the human anger inside herself that tore at the gentle boyish soul and the aggressive face of a girl that were her own.

At the same time, Joshi needed to find where she belonged, *and* find that book that was the kudzu's source! It had only been fifteen minutes since Joshi had knocked out the librarians, but it seemed like hours to Joshi. She needed to search more quickly, and not dwell on the books themselves when her friends' lives were at stake. Joshi picked up the chains of kudzu and spun them around, knocking books off of shelves in one swift motion that let her see the spines. There . . . right there! That one, that book, there! She picked up a dusty book with a pink spine that had an unusually large clump of kudzu extending from the middle page.

The kudzu was moving, growing, right out of the pages of the book in long leafy trails. Joshi drew her hockey stick, aimed, and whacked with the force of a Viking axe, right down the center of the book's binding. The covers went flying, and the kudzu receded and withered like old broccoli abandoned in a freezer. The title of the book was *Corruption of the Masses and the Young and Innocent: How to Exchange Your Soul for Fame and Money.* In bold letters under the title it said *Over 100 million copies sold!*

Joshi had thought the worst was over, but she was wrong, for at the doorway stood a librarian with a very sharp and giant toothpick in her hands like a spear, armed and ready.

"YOU! You destroyed the knowledge!" screamed the lady, furious with greed.

Joshi ran towards her, hockey stick out for battle, when the librarian took a piece of kudzu out of her nose and lit it on fire. "Take one step closer and this building will burn down and take every book with it!"

"You're the one who's destroying the knowledge!" Joshi yelled.

Fire and heat were especially hazardous to Joshi, who's inner spiritual element was water. Ioshi began to cry but the tears came from Joshi's eyes and flooded the room in fearsome waves that extinguished the small flame the librarian held. However, the librarian still had her toothpick weapon, and she charged at Joshi, had clouded vision from her tears, a cost for the water attack.

The librarian struck hard and Joshi had to dodge quickly. She had the disadvantage of not being able to see the points at which the weapons bashed against each other, and many times Joshi narrowly escaped being stabbed by an end of the toothpick. Exhausted from her tears and the fight, Joshi was budged into a corner and surrounded.

> *Ioshi, if my soul is let free, you and I will be equal, and the same, and I will protect you as you have me. But my friends, they need my energy to live. When I die, rip out my soul so they can use its stamina to get free of the trap. I'm sorry I will not*

fulfill my promise to protect you when we are equals in Heaven, when no one will be ashamed of my ashes that are the same substance as your wings.

At that critical moment, Joshi opened her eyes and did not see her guts spilling from her body as she expected, but instead saw Wakezashi fending off the librarian with a grappling technique and guard swing from the shiny wakezashi (a type of Japanese sword) in her hand. She helped Joshi to her feet. "Wakezashi's name ain't Wakezashi for nothin'!"

"I never knew you were a martial arts expert! You're terrific!"

"Well, it's an old hobby Wakezashi took up to put extra food on the table. Used to be really busy—pro chef, and bodyguard on the side."

That afternoon everyone in the gang was back in the World of Nevers and in good health.

Hitherforme had been gone all day walking beyond the horizon. "Joshi, I found this note for you. It was just sitting out there, in the middle of the Nothing-lands, waiting for someone to come and pick it up." Joshi thanked her and read the note:

Joshi, yeah, you, I'm talking to you, you tomboy ninja:

Someone is looking for you. If you do not look for the someone, no one will find you.

> *When no one finds you, someone gives up. You don't give up, so you go, ninja!*
>
> *Sometimes lost items are found in the places we've already searched a hundred times.*
>
> *Do not fear exploitation.*
>
> —*Pokey*

"Zippy, I need you to take me back to where I came from, right now, please." If the real world would accept her, she would remain there forever.

There is a difference
between confusion and
confusement.
I don't know what it is.

Chapter 15

Deleted Memory

Lukkar yanked open the second drawer of the file cabinet with his mouth. His teeth had grown longer, so he had been gnawing at a lot of things lately. The drawer had three clearly marked files in it, none of which were of any interest to him, except that one smelled like corn dogs. Lukkar sniffed again, but suddenly the files were no longer there, and he was no longer looking into a file cabinet.

Yoshi picked him up and scratched his ears. "You must be careful here. There are more dangers in the known than the unknown. The known is not always the truth, and even if it is, it is feared. And when it is not feared, it is ignored, and some hurt in ignorance."

Back on the floor again, Lukkar wanted to crawl under the bed and play with a sock he left there. He didn't see a bed to crawl under, but he did see what appeared to be similar to a sleeping bag with a design kind of like the one on Joshi's bed comforter. He crawled into the blankets on the floor because they looked snuggly and warm and smelled like Joshi. He stuck his muzzle under a bump in the fabric and smelled a sock—his sock. Life is good when one can find a missing sock.

Someone entered Yoshi's room. "Yoshi, you're back!" Her sister Risai sounded relieved.

Yoshi started to explain her absence from the semi-real world. "Yes, if that's what you call waking up in a different—"

Her sister's tone changed from happiness to worry. "Now that you're back you can disprove what's been said about you!"

"I don't care about gossip."

"No, what *relatives* have been saying about the gossip about you." Risai said.

"They want me to change myself, don't they?"

"But don't do it, Yoshi," said Risai, putting her arm on Yoshi's shoulder, "You're Jo-, I mean, you're Yoshi, unlike any other nonconformist, and even an individualist! But not in the public eye. People have been calling you a weird one for years, and our family paid no notice, till the rumors started saying you were a real psychopath, least-aways." Risai paused for a moment to catch her breath. "For many days you have not been wanted back by the relatives, and now they do, but only because they want to be able to show the neighbors that the rumors aren't true and that you are an average child."

"So they want me to change to keep up a reputation of the family? Even before I left whatever place this is people disliked us for being the mystery family with a noisy, bad-tempered home."

"Yoshi, the noises the Grumbly one makes—the neighbors think it's you."

"Mother's husband's been mad and warped for years, and he's the one who thinks I should change?"

"Yes, but do not change—pretend, like you did before your stories were exploited. Act the way the stupid Grumbly one wants you to, for sake of filial piety." Risai looked as though she might cry. Yoshi knew she had her best interests in mind. "When each day is over and no one can see you in the dark, write down everything you would have said and done that day if you'd been yourself, and make it as if you've lived an extra day, a much better day!"

Joshi thanked Risai for her advice and lay down on her floor-bed. Lukkar came out of a fold in the fabric and dropped a sock on her shoulder. "Thanks, Luk. I'd rather receive a sock from you than ten million yen from the Grumbly One."

⋆thud⋆ Yoshi covered her ears and then realized the noise was not from construction getting done on the building next door. She looked up, startled to see Wakezashi by her window.

Wakezashi also looked bewildered. "Why is the sky painted gray? Who could do such a thing, such a waste of time and colors."

Joshi agreed. "Some people poison the earth so they can live lavishly, but in exchange later generations, their offspring, must live in smog."

"Hellooo, Yo-Yo!" said Zippy, who appeared by the bedroom entrance and attempted to close a door that was already closed. "I've got something to make you smile. This new diet will make life a lot more flavorful!"

"No thanks. I hate diets. I've never been on one, and never will be," said Yoshi.

"I agree with you on that, but this diet is ex-cep-tion-al!" Zippy waved her hands in the air. "It's called the Zip-Zip and Yo-Yo diet. Eat chocolate when you're sad, to burst endorphins. Eat brain food when you're happy, like peanut butter, to help you put energy to good use. A blend of chocolate and peanut butter daily, plus meat and noodles is the perfect diet for anyone who wants to grow up to be a werewolf!"

"Thanks, Zippy. Now I know why the diet was named after me."

"What are are are endorphins?" asked Raski, who crawled out of the trash can in Yoshi's room.

"Endorphins are little husky puppies made of scientific matter living in your brain. When they are pepped up and pulling sleds, your brain is happy and functional. When they don't get the right kind of dog food to eat, which is called serotonin, they are still hyper up but not in a normal way. They spend time doing lots of activities besides pulling sleds, which produces a whole lot of brain activity for doing and thinking many things at once.

"However, when that happens not enough sleds are pulled, keeping the happy meter down, and the extra activities take up too much mental energy for normal thinking. That causes the brain to explore areas it normally wouldn't. A synthetic and prescribed dog food can then be fed to the puppies in the absence of serotonin. These are called happy pills. They're only used correctly if your doctor prescribes them. The happy pill dog food doesn't taste as good as the serotonin dog food, but it works almost as well."

Joshi imagined the sled-dogs in her brain working hard to pull a sled on a conveyer belt; thinking that they were working, but not actually getting anywhere. Raski imagined puppy dogs in his head pulling sleds at top speed while juggling balls on their noses, because surely his husky dogs must be extraordinarily efficient for his level of genius.

Qrsis was suddenly rearranging every item on Yoshi's desk, and Fjordka was pushing the buttons on the wall thermostat. Wakezashi played tag with Rainer and Raski in a room too small to adequately hold more than three people, which meant Yoshi was declared the safe base. Yoshi sat by herself, enjoying the company of friends. She was playing with her hand-painted wolf figurines, ignoring the fact that she was already twelve years old.

"Where's Jÿger?" she asked Zippy as she took a little wolf pup figuring and had it come out of its den. This would be its first view of life outside its den. It was now old enough to run around in the forest with the other wolves. The alpha female wolf licked the little one's fur and howled in approval. Other pack members came forward, bringing meat from a recent hunt.

"I told you that . . ." Zippy's sentence was cut off by the sound of a spoon being dropped. Somewhere in the apartment, a spoon had fallen to the ground with a resounding clang that reopened a stiff stillness, followed by a strong gust of noise pollution that rushed through the building and shook it like wind. All of the visitors from the World of Nevers were sucked away by the noise zephyr and tunneled back home through the Abyss. Zippy held onto the doorknob for a few seconds, fighting the suction long enough to say 'later' to Yoshi before being pulled away.

Yoshi sulked. Her only friends were gone, and the wicked noise that pierced the walls continued like a thousand people shouting for mercy, or a hundred children weeping. Because the sound of a spoon dropping shattered the stillness of enjoyable kaos. "I'm still here," said Ioshi in Yoshi's mind, and indeed Yoshi remembered Ioshi. She hugged a stuffed gray dog. Her room was filled with stuffed animals. Her heart beat faster and her head began to ache. The stuffed animals smiled at her with a gentleness that could not be found in human faces.

⋆Flick!⋆ Joshi turned on the radio. The happy kaotic stillness had been drowned out by dull, broken reality. She wanted to find another sound to shut out that ferocious dullness. "Today's weather is partly cloudy with a chance of *dingoes* coming in from the northeast. The temperature high is at the national average, so such a day is great for taking a stroll outside and *depicklizing pickles.* Tomorrow's skies are predicted to be even brighter than today's, with a short drizzle in the morning and sunny the rest of the day. It's the time of year that makes you say, 'Ahh, what nice *lederhosen I am wearing*!' And if that doesn't cheer you up, here's Hana, with the sports report up next."

"Hello, all you *supa'hiiroos*! The results are in from the latest *snail race* and the grand champion was *an iceberry mushroom* with a two year old horse named *I don't know what I'm looking for, but I'll know when I find it.* The grand prize, which included *a toilet plunger* and a golden, first place *toilet seat*, is estimated to be worth—*4.909* yen. When asked what would be done with the prize, *Jÿger*, the first-place jockey, responded, *'Remember when we fought in the Trojan War together?'* On the subject of *pogo-sticks* and *ping-pong*, all-star athlete, *Imp*, nicknamed *'Snarg'* by adoring fans has announced that he will be going into retirement this June in order to 'spend more time *watching his favorite martial arts soap opera, Udo and Yui.*

"Stay tuned for the entertainment news with *Yoshi Tokio*, reporting on the new movie release, *'I'm not Krazy'* starring *Shorty, Psycho Luris, and Ioshi*, and directed by leading film maker *Zippedity Zhong*." Tickets are selling fast, so much that the box office workers can only stand back and say *'I want my fight back!'*"

wizz The radio lost reception and went silent.

Yoshi heard a hand knocking on her bedroom door, and then many more hands knocking on her bedroom door. "You don't need to knock so much."

"Yoshi, I only knocked once. I think a part of you still hasn't come back yet . . . Anyway, this came in the mail for you." Risai handed her an envelope, statically shocking her as their hands touched for the brief moment. The return address on it was written in runic script. Yoshi reached for her boot but then realized she didn't need the paintbrush to read the runic letter inside.

Dear Yoshi,

I forgot what I was going to tell you, but I might as well say hi.

Sincerely but not sincere,

Joshi

Yoshi felt relieved that she wasn't the only one who'd forgotten something. There was something she was going to Joshi in response to the letter, but she'd also forgotten it already. On the other side of the paper was a letter written by Zippy, whom Joshi had assumed would be the one writing to her in the first place.

Dear Yoshi,

Thinking of you and of blue. Say hi to Pokey for me, will ya'?

Love Zippy

Stamped at the top of the page was the imprint from a rubber seal that said "From the office of the official toilet inspector." At the bottom of the page below Zippy's name everyone else she'd known from the World of Nevers had signed, except for Jÿger, who put a yellow dot sticker in place of his name, and Lukkar, who put a stamp of his pawprint, and Snarg, who singed a corner of paper with her fire breath, and Orange Fungus, who chewed off the other bottom corner of the paper, which left tiny tooth marks.

Yoshi sat at her desk and help up the paper under the lamp, searching it for clues like a little kid who thinks she's found a treasure map. There was nothing written in invisible ink, nor any words scratched out. Yoshi slid back in her chair. The wheels on the chair hit something on the floor, her hockey stick which lay under her desk. She hadn't realized it came back with her. To get it out of the way, she stowed it under her desk. One end reached the ground with a thump, and the other fell with a ⋆clang⋆ to where she'd shoved it out of her way. Only, thing is, carpeted floors do not go 'clang' like metal or hardwood does. She stomped her foot under her desk in the spot of the ⋆clang⋆. Yes, it went 'clang' many more times. A different type of material lay under the carpet.

On her hands and knees, Yoshi scooted under her desk and thumped the spot with her firsts. She felt around and noticed the rim of a square under the carpet. Something felt like a button poking out of the carpet. Yoshi remembered the last time an odd button had been found in a random place and resolved not to touch it. As she was getting back up, she put down her knee accidently on the hockey stick (for it was a small crowded room), which slid sideways over the button on the floor.

A square of carpeted floor swung open like a trapdoor, and by chance Yoshi fell right through it, hockey stick and all. She bumped down a tightly-packed stairway in a small corridor with a low-lying roof. At the bottom of the stairs was a small area that held a file cabinet. Yoshi had hardly been small enough to squeeze down the stairs, the only way in and the only way out, so how did a large file cabinet ever get down there?

The file cabinet was not like the one that she'd seen in the World of Nevers. It was bright aqua with alphabet magnets on it. "INK" was spelled out with some of the letters. Other magnets had complete words on them that strung together to make sentences. Yoshi had seen this style of magnets before, but never with such random words on them. One strand of magnets made this sentence "Know there is Abyss blue something not here." Another garble of magnets had words like *conjugation*, *endorphins*, *runaroundandpaint'em*, and *confusement*. Three drawers made up the filing cabinet, and the top one was shut tight with a combination lock.

Yoshi pulled open the two unlocked drawers. The middle one had files in it and the bottom one contained nothing but empty space. The first file in the middle drawer had "Pokey" written on the tab and next to it was stamped this message: "Character Data Change: See Next File for more Current Info." The next file had "Yoshi" written on it in Japanese. The remaining files after it were all connected at the sides in one tremendous file labeled "fragments." From Pokey to Yoshi to Joshi . . . Yoshi looked at a photo of Pokey and saw her younger self before a voluntary data change occurred. She imagined Pokey standing in line at the Character Data Center. While others asked to be rich or famous or both, Pokey asked to go where she'd always dreamed of going. She was to soon move with her family to a place far away from the dreamland that she believed could resolve her problems. Her request was granted, and she was far away from home, but not from the problems of home. Unlike the others wanting to change their information, Pokey carried no box of personality items under her arm, for she would exchange something much more precious: her memory.

Yoshi read through Pokey's file. She read of Pokey's many days alone at the swing set during fourth grade recess hour, and of how Pokey was a classroom politician, campaigns, speeches, debates and all. She had just begun to fit in at school and had made a few true friends when she found out her family would be moving to a place she did not want to go. School life had been getting more exciting and fun only to end soon with a new school she already did not like while home life had degraded to absolute misery. No wonder she wanted to forget and start over.

Yoshi had only been down in the secret room a few minutes, but it would only take just a little more time till she'd have to go do work in the form of errands or chores, and her sudden absence would stir up a lot of commotion from her family, especially since she had not been around the past few days while in the World of Nevers.

Yoshi closed the middle drawer and spun the dial of the top drawer's lock. It was the same kind as the locks on the P.E. lockers at school. She needed to start somewhere with trying to unlock it, so she thought of the default combination that came with all of the school's locks. She'd seen her P.E. coach reset the combinations for new locks.

If she started with the default numbers and increased the first digit by one each time, and then the second and third, she'd at least know what combinations she'd already tried. 10, spin to the right, 20, spin to the left twice, 30 spin to the right once . . . the first combination of numbers she tried was the default . . . ⋆snap⋆ and it actually worked! Maybe some things aren't too good to be true?

She released the lock and opened the top drawer, which contained a red book covered in cobwebs. Yoshi wiped of the cover and saw no title, so she opened it up where written on the inside cover was *The Problem Child's Bible.* It was a real Bible, its size a bit larger than her hand. A few old photographs fell out of the pages as she turned them. She did not recognize the people in them, but she felt that at one time she must have known their faces. She wished to know them again, so she started reading. There were shadows of tears from years past smudged onto the first few pages.

Pokey, did you not feel equal? Ioshi, did you not feel safe? A piece of paper, a book mark, fell out of the Bible. "He was too weak for this world, so the boy was taken to live with God where he watched over the child that inherited his spirit. When his wings had grown, he was called Johan, and Ioshi the gentle lion lived through Joshi the ravaged sheep."

Yoshi felt overwhelmingly inspired, so she ran back up the stairs and to her room window. She took out blue paint and thinned it before applying it to the tip of her Joshi paintbrush. She made long strokes on the upper glass of the window, tinting the glass so the sky looked blue. "I'm repainting the sky blue for you, Wakezashi."

Joshi turned around. Her room looked as it had when she was in the World of Nevers, and she looked like Joshi, only completely human. Her whole home and the world outside the window changed, becoming a neighborhood similar to the World of Nevers, but only more realistic. Her family and her were no longer Japanese people living in Japan. This was the world she had been living in but had neglected to see for many years.

Johan spoke. "To live in reality, you will have to accept it. You cannot wait for it to accept you, for I cannot guarantee that will ever happen. Will you try to live in this world—in God's world, with rules that are not your own?"

CHAPTER 16

Insert title here

"Hello, Joshi. I am Ms. K. Nice to meet you. I hear you like udon and ninjas."

That was the greeting of the psychotherapist sitting in front of Joshi. She reached out her right hand to shake, but Joshi inadvertently gave her a static shock. The lady in a business suit was neither smiling nor frowning, but she seemed pleasant and poised sitting upright in an arm chair, similar to the one Joshi sat in across from her. Even while wearing stiff pants and a starchy jacket Ms. K. seemed comfortable and casual with the sleeves of her buttoned shirt rolled up. Her hair was short and wavy as if the wind had blown it into position. She wore no jewelry and could not be any older than twenty-seven.

"Why don't you tell me a little about yourself, Joshi?"

"My blood type is O negative. I was born in the year of the sheep and in the hour of the snake. I have passed seven grade levels at school, not counting kindergarten. I don't have a job and I live with my family. I have a little sister named Risai, no, I mean Lise." Joshi had forgotten for a moment that she was not Yoshi and in her forgetfulness had used the Japanese form of her sister's name. "And Lise was born an hour after me in the hour of the rabbit, my brother's sign is boar, and that's why Anji, Grethe, and Dagmar say Rollo is so bor-ing . . ."

"No, I want to hear about you personally. Please tell me about you, and the things you like and dislike."

"Okay, well, I like things that are blue, and I don't like things that are pink. I also like rocks and mopeds. I collect rocks and I wish I could collect mopeds. One day I'm going to be a professional ninja and major in martial arts at college, and I also want to publish graphic novels, explore the world, and invent something that makes it possible for animals with limited vision to see all colors of the rainbow spectrum with human-like eyesight."

"Very ambitious, for someone your age."

"I have a lot of time to think because people ignore me so much, I can do whatever I want. Sometimes I think I don't really exist."

"Well, you know as they say, if you believe in something, it will be real."

"Yeah, and unfortunately the rest of the world has that figured that it works the other way too, so they know what to do to get rid of me. I'll just disappear into the earth."

Miss K. leaned in a little closer and lowered her voice. "If the rest of the world didn't exist, would you believe in yourself?"

"I don't know. But if I forgot everything I was taught before it went away, I would. They taught me I was slow and dumb and a pain to everyone. They wouldn't let me keep my friends, so I had to go away and stare at the wall for hours. And when the world ends it will be my fault for not doing more in my lifetime."

"Who exactly is this 'they?'"

"They are them. They have always been there, and they follow one around, watching, exploiting . . . they know everything and remind me of it."

Miss K. patted Joshi on the head, and Joshi liked it. She smirked through her tears that she hadn't even realized were rolling down her face.

"It gets better if I say it's all funny. I could get up in the middle of class at school and walk right out of the classroom and no one would notice. In the hallways, people walk so close to me, just like they can't see me, and trample me in an uncrowded hall with lots of space because they can't see me, because I know if they did they would move over and give me space to walk. At home I could sit in the very room where my parents are talking disgracefully about me behind my back, and nine out of ten times they would never know I was there." Joshi inflected her voice to give humor to her words. She laughed a little, but not loudly.

"Do not be ashamed of the skill you have acquired." said Miss K. "Some will see you, as I see you now. A few people will see you and try to get others to see you and respect you, but others might never respect you, for it is hard to believe in something that you cannot see with your eyes."

"I can't see myself with my own eyes, and neither can anyone else see themselves . . . does that make any sense to you, Miss K.?"

"There are those who cannot see what they believe, but still believe strongly enough to see it in their minds." Miss K. maintained direct eye contact with Joshi. "I have my own secrets, Joshi. I am not a real psychotherapist. I am a master of ninjutsu, and I lead my own Shinobi clan. Will you join?"

Meanwhile, in the World of Nevers, Zippy was organizing her latest project. Raski, Emune, Rainer, and a dozen other boys recruited from the sign-up sheet stuck to a wall of the arcade, stood side by side in line giving strict obedience and attention to Zippy, who walked back and forth in front of them with a long stick she held behind her back.

"Do all of you understand what you have volunteered for?"

"Sir, no sir," the boys replied in unison.

"It will be fierce and competitive. Only the tough will make it." By now many of the boys were sweating in nervous anxiety. "It will be more challenging than any competition you've ever entered before. Prepare yourselves for . . ." Zippy broke into a smile and twirled around, waving the stick in the air in excitement. "The first-annual Zip-Zip's Male Beauty Pageant!" Several dumb looks popped up across the faces of the boys, most wanting to go home by now. "There will be only one winner, only one champion who will claim the title of Mr. Stupendous!" The sweat drops rolling down the boys' faces grew larger.

One boy raised his hand. "Um, Zippy,"

Zippy shot him a glaring look and the boy corrected his mistake.

"Um, Sir, um, do we really have to do this?"

"Of course not," said Zippy, smirking, thinking of the several schemes up her sleeve, "You can just quit now and skedaddle off as a sissy who wasn't good enough to face up to the big guys. You'll just want to kick yourself later for missing all the fun." The boy who asked the question put his hand down and stayed in line.

Zippy strutted over to a break in the line where no one stood. A yellow dot sticker was stuck to the floor where one eligible participant should have been. "JŸGER!"

Jÿger was running his usual round of package deliveries. He stopped for a moment because he heard something that sounded like someone off in the distance was yelling. Oh, well, he couldn't figure out what it was, so he continued on his way, pulling Imp behind him in the kiddie wagon. Jÿger didn't know why, but all of a sudden he had a feeling that he should kick himself.

"Oh, well," said Zippy, fanning away the fumes that came from her anger, "we'll put in a replacement. Has anyone seen Orange Fungus?"

"Remember, Joshi," said Miss K. as Joshi left to find Orange Fungus, "Everything said in this room stays here."

Zippy skipped across the stage. During rehearsal, after weeks of training, the boys whispered back and forth to each other.

"Who do you think will win?"

"The sherbet-colored rabbit has a good chance."

"If Zippy's stuck on herself, she might choose Emune because he looks a lot like her."

"Raski's wearing lederhosen because he thinks it will help."

Orange Fungus, however, was disqualified from participating in the contest for disappearing in the middle of rehearsal, so he was promoted and reassigned to the position of assistant judge.

Joshi opened the door to the psychotherapy office. It seemed like she had left it only recently, although it had been three weeks since she last talked to Miss K.

"How goes it Joshi?"

Joshi was tired, grateful that her seat was so comfortable. "I'm just glad you didn't ask me 'How are you?' because I never know how to answer that question. I know that things aren't going so good, but why would that be anybody's business? I also don't like being asked to reflect on how bad it's affecting me, 'cause I don't want to worry about what will not change." Joshi laughed, and then made her voice somber. "Shinobi Master, why would my family be ashamed of me?"

Miss K. said nothing but looked straight into Joshi's eyes and into her brain. *They see something in you that you can't see, and that kind of potential scares them,* said Ninja Master K. telepathically. She patted Joshi on the head. "I used to be a karate instructor, but I still practice Skandinsword and berserking battle technique today. Would you like to learn some of each?" Joshi's eyes shined so bright she did not need to give an answer. Regardless, Ninja Master K. already knew the answer she would give.

After kicking, blocking, punching, and shuffling around with pretend shields, they sat down again. "A good workout helps raise endorphins." said the master of ninjas.

"What are endorphins?"

"Endorphins are complex chemical-hydroxylades made of polyhelxic data similar to RNA, or ribonucleic acid, that combust futon-oil and carbopeptide into a bacterium vacuole that generates kinetic waves from the endothermically-transmitted molecular polar particles of the ventialting ribosomes of the brain fluids to emit endorphic membranes of sub-ionic tissue that stimulate the brain to feel happy." Ninja Master K., not being a real science expert or psychotherapist, had an explanation just as confusing as Zippy's sled-dog story. So she knew just as much as Joshi did on the topic; endorphins had something to do with chemicals of the brain and that they make a person feel happy. Wasn't a futon a piece of furniture?

"Why would my family be ashamed of me?" Joshi remembered her original concern.

"Little ninja, you did nothing to deserve it, but you have a disease. Your family doesn't understand this disease, but they can't even begin to understand it until you do. It's sometimes deadly and is genetic. Your older relatives know you have the disease and sometimes they blame you for bringing it into the family, as they think of it. But they are wrong because they do not understand it. The disease actually started generations ago, and even your parents may have it and not know it."

"Are any of my relatives at risk of dying?"

"No, Joshi, they are in much better condition than you, so far as I can tell. Keep fighting the battle, Joshi, and you'll be fine too."

The battle? Could the Shinobi Master know somehow about the stormy battles Zippy told her about? A storm inside her was a battle.

Joshi sat at her desk at home, trying to read. The *Blue Vikings* magazine was very enjoyable, but the trapdoor in the floor distracted her. For a few minutes she doubted that the experience had even happened while she was awake, but curiosity prevailed and so did the reasoning that finding such a spot would offer a quick escape from the awful noises of her relatives screaming at each other. She knelt below her desk and felt around.

A familiar voice startled her. "I'm back!!!" Hearing Zippy's voice made Joshi lift up her head suddenly, which caused her to bump it on the bottom of her desk. Zippy was impatient. "What're you doing? Come, come, come!"

Having no choice in the matter, Joshi felt sucked herself being sucked into a toilet and surrounded by the sea of blue in the toilet waters of the Abyss. The trap door's secrets would have to wait.

She landed in a large auditorium where she could see no one but Zippy. Zippy blew a whistle and yelled, "Come on out!" A dozen or more boys rushed onto the stage and formed three rows. "This is a male beauty pageant. I've organized this all for you, Joshi, so you can be the judge!" Joshi doubted that Zippy's only reason to boss around a bunch of boys was to cheer up a friend who did not like beauty pageants.

Zippy and Joshi sat down on the front row where Orange Fungus joined them, climbing out from his hiding place under the seats. "The assistant judge wants to begin now." Zippy spoke for the rabbit who only seemed to notice the carrot he was eating. With each bite his fur began to turn from green to orange. Joshi realized she had never seen Orange Fungus eat a carrot before. On the other side of her Zippy was poking her left shoulder.

"But, Zippy, I don't know anything about judging pageants. It's really an area of your expertise anyway."

"So?"

"I don't really approve of pageants for either gender because they base the prizes on looks when all contestants look the same with fake looks."

The boys on stage all gasped, shocked at such blunt news.

"True, my friend, but perhaps you shall find this one to be different. I've found a new judge—me!" Zippy pointed to herself and smiled as wide as her mouth could stretch. "And I've also found a new participant too—you!" Zippy leaned over and hugged Joshi very tightly. Then she said the words Joshi dreaded. "We're waiting, Ioshi!" Ioshi jumped up from his seat and ran backstage to prepare. He knew that if he didn't follow Zippy's orders he'd be kicking himself later. There was something very persuasive—or very ominous—about receiving orders from Zippy.

The pageant started with a modeling portion that began with occupational wear (each category had been made up by Zippy). Raski had a toilet plunger on top of his head. He was hoping to impress Zippy by looking like a plumber. His original plan was to dress up as a rocket scientist, but some people told him it wasn't believable enough. Rainer walked out in a chef's costume because it was the only one he already had suitable for that portion of the pageant. To make up for a rather normal costume, he did back flips as he went across the stage.

Emune was a brain surgeon. Ioshi came out in a ninja uniform, but he said he was a psychotherapist. Ioshi didn't know how the word "psychotherapist" suddenly came to mind when asked what his occupation was. Zippy loudly expressed her disappointment that no one came dressed as a multicolored alien dog.

"I didn't know that was an occupation," Ioshi complained.

"Duh! What do you think I do all day? It takes hard work doing what I do!"

The second modeling segment was for evening wear. Raski came out wearing pajamas with a teddy bear tucked under his arm.

"Finally, someone knows the meaning of the term!" Zippy applauded.

Rainer wore a formal masculine kimono and Emune had a clock set on eight p.m. taped to his t-shirt. Ioshi disappeared back stage.

Talent was the next portion. Many boys tried to sing or tell jokes. Rainer performed a Norweigan berserk-kung-fu routine, the first of its kind Zippy had ever seen. Raski tried to balance a chair on his nose, but ended up breaking both the chair and his nose. Emune sat in the middle of the stage and attempted to read Zippy's fortune. Zippy didn't allow Ioshi to take a game console on stage for winning a round of video games, so he used his hands as puppets to act out a story he made up about a snail with wings that wanted to fly over the moon.

Interviewing was the last round of the competition. Zippy had a question for each participant.

"What would your first action be if you were president?

"I I would immediately resign so so so you could could take office." said Raski, trying to suck up for a better chance of winning.

"What is the best topping for a double cheeseburger?"

"Cheese." said Emune

"If you had a pet polar bear, what would you name it?"

"Iceflake—a combination of icicle and snowflake." said Rainer

"If you were me interviewing you, what question would you ask?"

"Why are you so darn good looking?" said Ioshi with a laugh, not taking seriously what he'd just said.

Zippy stood up on the stage behind a podium. "I shall now announce the winner! I now crown Ioshi Mister Stupendous! Ioshi is such a beautiful boy! He shall receive the grand prize of . . ." the boys standing at the back of the stage 'oo'ed and' aww'ed. "This sash that says *Mister Stupendous*!" The next moment everyone was applauding and excited, except for Ioshi. The other contestants lifted him up in the air and cheered over and over again.

Shinobi Master...
I am not worthy of entering the realm you speak of.
My student,
you are already there
and you have always been there.

CHAPTER 17

Watch out, Mr. Fuzzyhead

"Pick an item, any item."

Joshi stuck her hand into the cardboard box of objects in front of her. The box sides were high enough that from her seat in the arm chair she could not see into it, just reach inside. Following the instructions of her wannabe-psychotherapist, she moved her hand around the items till she touched something that felt blue and pulled it out.

"Very good," said Ninja Master K. "Now I want you to tell me how you are like that blue kitchen timer."

Joshi hadn't expected that kind of question, but she immediately answered. "People think that I am quiet all the time because I'm quiet when out in public, but at the moment they least expect it, my long fuse is cut short, and I surprise them with anger. I'm not allowed to speak very often, but when I am, I make the most of it, contrary to many opinions."

"Where are you when you shout?"

"Anywhere, anytime. When they start screaming, I want to yell back, and sometimes I do. They start it and when it gets to be too much to handle, I yell back."

"So it's *them* again?" asked Miss K.

Shinobi Master, do you believe that I am the one disturbing everyone else?"

Zippy was enjoying a new game as she skipped on one foot on the sidewalk outside the arcade. She spun around five and a half times and pointed. Following the path of her pointer finger, she saw a frog sitting on the branch of a tree. "I am like that frog because we both like sitting in trees." Another go at it and Zippy was facing a leaf. "Both of us have veins and change color—you depending on the season, me depending on the species I am." Repeating the spinning process, Zippy tumbled closer to the pavement and looked up. "I am like that yellow dot sticker on the window because . . ." Zippy took a deep breath in the chasm of her mind, a thought so deep that some refer to it as a 'thinker.'

Zippy's eyes lit up like fireworks. "We both represent sunshine and the best of anything a person could like. The dot sticker for Jÿger and me for Pokey." She sighed and her voice trembled. "And neither of us successfully serves our purpose. Another similarity—we are both man-made."

"Hello, Joshi. It's time to remove those zits!"

"No, ma'm, please . . ." Joshi begged the dermatologist. "Don't make me conform to conformity! I will not let my face be zapped and dematerialized for the dumb sake of beauty. I don't want to be beautiful! I want to stay zitty, really! I need my zits to look smart and intellectual so I don't lose myself. Besides, the pimples bring color to my pale face . . ."

"Relax. If it's the pain you're worried about, just say so—"

Joshi continued her rant. "Believe me! The last thing I want is to blend in with a crowd. I want to keep my skin natural, even if it is sweaty and oily, so what if I bathe less often than other people, it's all about being happy with myself, right?"

"This procedure has been ordered by your parents, and I, for one, agree—"

"Because it gives you money, like how the orthodontist tells everyone they have crooked teeth so he can score more dough from braces." Joshi couldn't believe she just said that. But because she did just say that, she would have to face the consequences of ticking off a professional with sharp tools aimed at her face.

The dermatologist laughed. This kid had one unusual outlook on things. "If I don't do this your skin will be unhealthy and your face will scar."

"Washing my face every day is good enough for me . . ."

"But not for the hormones that have started to pop up."

"Fine, for sake of parental piety, like everything else I'm obligated to do, I'll hold still and let you begin. But what will you use to suck out my zits, anyway?"

"A spoon." The dermatologist laughed again.

ZAP *SLICE* *SPLATTER* Bloodiness and gore. Joshi didn't scream. She'd never had the ability to scream. But that didn't stop her from panicking.

"Hej, you lied! That wasn't a spoon, it must have been a spork!!!!" Joshi yelled. Cautiously she poked the sore spots on her face as if she were tampering with a wired bomb.

Joshi walked out into the waiting room and lobby area after her appointment. She still felt numb in her forehead. Classical music played softly over a radio and people were seated in plastic chairs reading magazines. How could these people willingly come to this place of shock and doom? How could they just relax and wait for zit zapping destruction?

A few people looked up from their reading to stare at the kid standing still in the doorway who wore a horrified look on her face. An office assistant scooted around Joshi because an attempt to get her to move was unsuccessful.

"Pssst." Joshi heard the sound as distinctly as a dog responds to a dog whistle. "Over here, Joshi." Joshi regained a sense of what was going on around her and moved out of the doorway, much to the office assistant's relief. Joshi tried to follow the voice to whoever was calling her, but she was very directionally challenged and went in circles around the entire room trying to find a familiar face. Ready to give up and admit she was hearing things, Joshi headed for the exit door. She was pushing it open when . . . *WHAM! A person sitting near the door had extended her foot and tripped Joshi.

"Whoops, my bad. So, they call you 'Joshi the kid'?"

"With all respect, it's none of your business . . . and my nickname's 'tomboy ninja' anyway."

The person who tripped her, a girl with dark hair and lime green sunglasses lowered the *Skrive* magazine that had come up above her nose. Joshi wanted very badly to punch that nose, but she knew restraint would be wise because Zippy might be her best chance to escape a place like that without further humiliation.

"What's new, Zippy? Hmm, those sunglasses do match your green antennas reappearing out of your head."

"Hee-hee. I like playing the part of punk, but it's not as fun as being the cute but demanding brat." Zippy winked. "I think we should go for a walk."

Zippy and Joshi headed down the hall of the medical center, which was decorated to resemble the outdoors, complete with lamp posts lined up in the middle of the carpet pathway, which was a green leaf print with blue and brown lines like tree roots winding through parts, and murals building exteriors on the wall. The ceiling was painted in clouds that Joshi could get her thoughts lost in. The hallways were such a contrast tothe dermatologist's office. She watched the clouds as she passed them, but soon she thought she saw a cloud drift past her before she could walk past it, and then another. She looked around, Zippy walking beside her and humming. They were no longer at the medical center. They were in the World of Nevers.

Zippy tugged gently at Joshi's sleeve and she stopped walking. Zippy pressed her face up against the glass of a toy store window. "It's not there anymore" she said with a whimper. Joshi looked in the glass display. It was a shop she'd glanced in at before, the one that once advertised a pogo stick. The pogo stick was not there and the platform it had stood on remained empty. "Imagine the places you could go on a pogo stick!" beamed Zippy. She squinted her eyes. "Look, the sign for it is still there. It's just invisible, that pogo stick."

"Is there anything you'd want more than a pogo stick, Zippy?"

"Yep."

"What?"

"It's a zip-zip secret."

"Okay."

"No, Joshi, you're not supposed to say 'okay' when someone tells you it's a secret. You're supposed to nag me about it till I give in and make you wish you hadn't asked."

"Thanks for warning me ahead of time; now I never will." Joshi said without any change in tone.

"Don't look so relieved, Joshi. *You* have a secret and I'm going to get it out of you."

"What? I seriously don't know what you're talking about."

Joshi heard an interruption in her brain, and it wasn't Zippy's voice. "I know you can't be responsible for the noise from your house. Ninja Apprentice, you have a mission."

"Ms. K.! I mean, Shinobi Master K!" Upon identifying the voice, the World of Nevers around her, including Zippy, stood still like a video on pause. A bright blue and silver moped sped down the road and pulled up next to Joshi. "Get on," said the Ninja Master K., who tossed Joshi a helmet. "Your mission is waiting."

Joshi enjoyed the ride and imagined what it would be like to drive her own moped someday. All too soon the fun, windy ride was over and they stopped inside a cave of snow. Nowhere else Joshi had seen was this abstract, not even anything she'd seen in the World of Nevers. Everything around had impossibilities. Joshi and Ms. K.'s shadows were alone. Items filled the place without having any shadows of their own shadow: living plants made of wires, rock formations in a speedy process of reverse erosion, a thesaurus that claimed *cool* was the wrong way to spell *kewl* . . . and a plain wooden easel.

"Your task is to tell me where we are." said Ninja Master K.

Joshi scampered around quickly and stealthily, as a ninja should. Every detail was to be examined. She was not in the Abyss or the World of Nevers, and if there was one place this place was not, that would be reality.

Joshi stepped up to the easel. A canvas and paints appeared along with her rune-written 'Joshi' paintbrush.

She began to paint a scene from her home neighborhood. As her paint strokes neared the edge of the canvas, it enlarged itself to give her space, as if the painting could expand as far as she kept painting. When Joshi set down her paintbrush, the scene faded from the canvas, which shrunk, and her art reappeared translucently projected as a layer all around her on the walls and floor and everything between them and herself, the painted neighborhood magnified to the size the scene would be in reality. The only big difference was that the image was upside down.

"Why is it that way?"

"This place always does that because it is necessary for one who is not in it to see things that way," said Miss K.

"Have I possibly been here before?"

"How would you expect me to know that?" said Ms. K., who in her mind thought to herself, *Yes, Joshi, You have been here before but you've never seen it like it is now.*

Joshi watched her footsteps disappear into plain ground. On plain stone she left imprints from her footsteps, which dissolved like a fingerprint made on jello. Joshi mixed all of the paint colors together, trying to make the color black. If she made black, she could see what the colors around her would be reflected as in the darkness of the color, changing color frequencies by painting. It was something that would not help her find any answers, but she was interested in seeing the true frequencies of the color scheme around her, being an artist and all that creative-ish stuff.

But the paint colors when evenly blended did not make black. A puddle of Joshi-color paint remained, the color Joshi had seen before that no one else had, the color of Joshi's soul. This could be a big hint to the answer of Ninja Master K.'s question.

"I would like to guess the answer, Shinobi Master."

"A guess? Not a theory or hypothesis or educated prediction?"

Joshi sulked. Yeah, a guess. She was going to ask Miss K. if she was inside Miss K.'s thoughts.

A small husky dog came out from nowhere and ran past the two of them in the snowy cave.

"No, Shinobi Master, I *know* where we are now. We are inside my brain."

"Yes, indeed, my young ninja."

"So . . ." said Zippy as she and Joshi walked along the street, "That was a really kewl secret!"

Joshi had no idea why time had suddenly resumed in the World of Nevers or what Zippy knew about what just happened.

A nearby trash can tipped over and rolled in front of them and crashed with a bang into the wall of a building. The lid fell off and an arm extended out of it to pull the lid back on. Zippy crept over to the trash can and pulled the lid away from Raski.

"I I should be be going now."

"No, you should stay and chat with Zippy," said Zippy in her cute but cruel voice.

"Um, uh uh, right, of of course! I meant meant after I stay and and and chat with with Zippy."

"How much of our conversation did you hear?"

Raski turned bright red. "I already already know all all all all all all of what you said said. But to to to make up up up for me me eavesdropping, I'll I'll I'll I'll tell you one one of my my secrets."

"I love secrets!" said Zippy, "As soon as they are broken, it means I have to find more secrets to keep . . . until they break!"

Raski cleared his throat and then spoke straightforwardly as if he were reading from a dialogue. "I have a talent for keeping memories. Many years ago I got lost in the desert. I survived only by thinking of legendary dingo stories I'd heard, and my ambition to catch a dingo became my motivation to survive."

Something was changing inside of Raski. Joshi couldn't tell if it was a good something or a bad something.

Raski kept speaking in grammatically-correct sentences. "Since then, I've always wanted to be around people, no matter how they treat me, because I need them to feel safe, even if I am the dunce of the group. Even people I dislike are better than none."

Joshi felt just the opposite, personally.

Raski continued. "I know I have a one-track mind, but it keeps people from thinking of me as a threat. Sometimes

I have nightmares that Orange Fungus has kidnapped me and dragged me into the desert—"

"Get to the point, Mr. Fuzzyhead." said Zippy, grabbing Raski's tie.

"I recognized Joshi before I met her. What I mean is I have a memory of her."

"How?" Joshi asked.

"I remember being on a playground with lots of other kids. I saw a swing set near the end of the playground in front of the fence that divided the playground from the junkyard. No one ever swung there because they can't stand the smell from the dumpsters and trash piles in the junkyard. I saw someone swinging there, as she had every day of recess, a girl that looked like Joshi, a younger Joshi." Raski's voice sounded unlike his own, but somehow it became familiar to Joshi.

"That's it? That's the memory?" said Zippy, unsatisfied with such a 'secret.' She loosened her grip on Raski's tie and he ran off again.

Joshi didn't say anything. She was deep in a sea of thought. Raski had seen a glimpse of her reality, her real world. Could he have seen more of that real world, even if she was not a part of it? Or perhaps he used to live in reality as she did.

"Help!" Joshi heard Emune's voice coming from the Abyss.

"We must go, Zippy."

Emune was sobbing, his hands covering his head as he sat on a blue tree stump on the ground.

"What's your problem?" Joshi blurted. Zippy nudged Joshi for her unintentionally rude comment.

"I mean, what's up with you?" Joshi tried again to express concern, but still sounded nosy without trying to be. "What I'm trying to say is, why so sulky?" Joshi was out on strike three for social infectivity.

Zippy took charge of the conversation after Joshi's social failure. "Feeling sadder than blue?" Zippy asked Emune.

"Told was I that which being happen will world end because reality not happy so is now, nations fall off earth not defended allies by are, world falling apart is. Was I told people forget good is what."

"So you have heard from someone that the entire earth, and this space too, will burst into pieces because nations will not aid the cause of right." translated Joshi, heartbroken to hear that the troubles of her reality were penetrating into even the peaceful souls of those who did not live in it.

"Therefore, Emune, do you think something like duct tape could help pull the earth together?" Zippy proposed. This time Joshi was the one who knew how to talk about the situation.

"Duct tape be if helpful when can force in come help to save."

"So this duct tape is a spiritual substance people are missing." Joshi resolved.

"If we pull the dimensions of earth together, we will have helped create a new universe. We should not end the world, but think of its second coming." Emune said, speaking more clearly than ever before. "Johan told me this, and it's what I believe."

"Belief is good," said Lukkar, poking his head out of Joshi's hood.

Everything around Joshi blacked out. "Joshi . . ." said Ms. K. the Shinobi Master, "You have just discovered a reason to stay in where you came from: to save your reality and the earth surrounding it, and to return to where you came from, before you were placed on a physical land."

"But what will happen to the World of Nevers if I abandon it?"

Zippy trudged through the swamp of a bathroom. She opened a medicine cabinet and threw out item after item as she searched for something she had lost many times before. It was something Joshi saw little value in, but held its relevance to Zippy's cause. A bath sponge, a rubber duck, and a snorkeling mask flew across the room before Zippy spotted something that might be of value. She had grabbed a medicine bottle and was about to hurl it behind her when she saw the label: 'PRESCRIPTION for ★★★★★, antidepressant, take one daily.'

"What is this doing in here?" Zippy shrugged as she wondered out loud. "I wonder how long Joshi's been missing her happy pills. Maybe she needs them for something." She put the medicine bottle in her pocket and pulled out more stuff until she found just what she was looking for, a roll of duct tape. "Better get started!"

CHAPTER 18

I'm Not Krazy

Orange Fungus jumped out of the toilet and hopped over to Zippy, who was lounging on the couch on her stomach, her feet kicking the air as she wrote her thoughts down on a piece of paper she ripped out of Joshi's journal.

Dear diary,

If I had a boyfriend, he would have blue hair and blonde eyes.

Zippy took a moment to laugh out loud and continued writing.

Now you know why I don't have a boyfriend.

Zippy patted Orange Fungus, who burped, revealing a slip of paper on his tongue. She took the handwritten note from Orange Fungus's mouth and gasped. "What's that, my fungi-friend? Fjordka and Qrsis need me? For what? Yeah, I'll be right there, buddy."

Zippy jumped into an astronaut jumpsuit (because you don't just *stand* in a *jump*suit) and plummeted down the toilet. Orange Fungus curled up on the toilet lid and fell asleep.

Joshi couldn't hold in her curiosity any longer. "Emune, take me to where you saw reality." Emune emitted a blue light, and soon Joshi was standing in a dark, shallow chamber with newspapers scattered around an aqua green file cabinet. Knowing what awaited within it, Joshi opened the file cabinet's second drawer, the drawer with the character profiles in it. Only now they weren't character profiles in the large folder marked "fragments." There were stories in stapled stacks, sitting in files designated by names, including such as "Hitherforme", "Emune", and "Qrsis"—recognizable names. Joshi read the papers one by one. Her favorite was a story titled *Rainer the Hibachi Chef,* an exciting mystery tale about Rainer as a hibachi chef at a Norwegian sushi bar who had to defeat unknown sneaky robbers who stole raw fish from the stock. Another great artifact was about *Wakezashi and the Robot Quest,* an excerpt:

> *Wakezashi lifted a sword and struck the enemy flag into the ground. If she was quick enough, three hundred thousand factory-working humanoid robotical units could be saved from ruthless slaughter. To destroy*

your own good creation was a terrible feat, and despite of that the owner of a corporation was going to reward programmed personalitized microchipped people, geniuses of the future, with a punishing death for their existance. One robot stepped out of the shivering building puffing out wisps of factory smoke, standing away from the rest. "Why don't the others fight for themselves? Don't they want a chance at life?" Wakezashi questioned the one. "They want to live, but they do not know how." said the one. "I can only come forward because my emotion-system has adapted to accept a new challenge, the feeling of courage."

The robot extended her hand. "Fjordka Interprises" was stamped on it. "When any group of people fights, even in self-defense, others shudder and fear they are violent. But when a group is erased from history, others say 'Oh, how weak they must have been.' People were not created to be used, nor to be destroyed. People were meant to live. But sometimes the only way to live is to die for something that deserves to live." Wakezashi bowed her head upon hearing such truth. "Fjordka, can you build three forts? I am not so strong with lifting things." Fjordka nodded and built four, to the best of her numberless ability.

The next story was made up completely of sketches and had no words at all. She saw Lukkar howling with wolves and traveling all around the world with a bamboo plant, Emune, strapped to his back. Joshi could imagine every character in their own story as the same people they were today. She imagined Wakezashi coming home from a battle and turning on the TV to watch another episode of the *Udo and Yui Ninja Soap Opera.*

"Pokey" was the signature of each handwritten story scratched on college-ruled notebook paper. Joshi read until there was only one folder left and it held the name she was most curious about: Zippedity Zhong. She did not know where the folders for Jÿger, Imp, and Raski could be, but they quickly floated out of her mind as she indulged herself in the Zippy story, titled *Zip-Zip and Poke-Poke Adventures.* Here is an excerpt:

> *Two fearless foes faced each other, evading the wind that blew so fiercely into their souls, one a human child, the other a person with a canine's heart. They swerved with the waves of ice crashing in with the wind, deflecting and striking blow after blow. One held a katana, the other a double-axe. "How come you have to be the person I wanted to be?" Pokey yelled in fury.*
>
> *"Because you created me that way! You wanted an adversary because you are miss perfect all the time! Everyone liked you, and you didn't like them for not seeing yourself, when you hate yourself! I don't even need to try to hate you because even without any orders to I've known you are a foul brat, owns nothing, wants the world, and cannot even handle her own wishes!"*

"You were devious from the beginning! It was you who cursed my life! You didn't care about anything but drinking out of the toilet! You weren't even good as an opponent, just a rival who didn't want the challenge I needed. You told me lies, that I could be stronger in another dimension and carry it to earth with me! An opponent is supposed to be your role, not someone who's trying to take over my mind! I caught you at it, and you purposely knocked me out to read my thoughts! I let you be so we could have an even match, but instead you create nightmares so I can have no peace!"

Zippy struck down Pokey, her own master. "You wanted an adversary but didn't admit it was too much for you to handle. You may have won every debate at school and every fist fight with me, but my words claim your throat. You'll get what you want! Become like me. I shall expel you across the ocean. Oh, and don't take it personally that I have a flare for mind-warping, this doggie has instinct, and you don't want to admit you have lost everything to an opponent you chose to create!

I lied to you because it's not fighting with you that I want, it's something else that I cannot have, and never will. Next time you create a friend, put them on your side of the battle. If you have a right to your wishes, then why can't I have a right to destroy what's not right, like people like you! You will never amount to anything, and I hope your heart explodes before you get the chance to screw up again!"

Qrsis came forward out of the shadows and slipped a paintbrush into one of Joshi's boots. She pitied her, not for foolishness, but for having too many brains, and not enough emotions. "T-a-k-e space C-a-r-e."

A folded piece of paper fell out of Zippy's folder. DISCLAIMER: ALL STORIES ARE COMPLETELY FICTIONAL AND ARE NOT BASED ON REAL-LIFE EVENTS. ALL CHARACTERS ARE FRAGMENTS OF LEFTOVER IMAGINATION THAT HAVE LIVED THROUGH THE FLOW OF INK, I'M NOT KRAZY. NO CHARACTERS INVOLVED IN THE FRAGMENT FILES ARE REAL PEOPLE. THE TEST FOR POKEY'S REALITY OF A PERSON IS THAT A LIVING CREATURE IN EXISTENCE WILL EMIT A STATIC SHOCK, IN MOST CASES. THESE CREATURES ARE KNOWN AS NONEXISTMENTS AND HELP SHOULD BE SAUGHT IMMEDIATELY IF ONE SHOULD INVADE YOUR LIFE.

Joshi trudged through the swampy bathroom over to the toilet. She looked into her reflection in the water and made a wish for Zippy. She tossed an arcade token into the toilet bowl (because coins are coins, right?).

A second person's reflection appeared in the toilet water. "If you want to make your dreams come true, maybe you should stop peeing in the wishing well," said Zippy.

It was a remarkably efficient wishing well if it could summon the person Joshi was thinking of within an instant!

"I read about you and Pokey," said Joshi, "How you tormented each other . . ." Joshi couldn't look Zippy in the face.

"I came back to you because it was my fault. I put more scars on your mind when you already had many. I didn't know that I was hurting myself too, by putting a scar in my heart. I'm not sure how, but one day I looked at the sky and felt so lonely. I also felt that I had cursed a person whom I was meant to help. You didn't mean for me to help you, just fight you, but obviously someone else did."

"I think the reason Pokey, I mean—I, hated you, was because I wanted to be your friend, and I wasn't used to wanting friends. I was confused and afraid because I didn't know how to handle positive emotion. . . . Do you think my pain is not real?" Joshi asked Zippy.

"No, but you still feel it, even when you know that, right? A headache and a chaotic heart, no, a *kaotic* heart. What's it like to feel pain, pain that does exist?" For once there was a question only Joshi had the answer to.

"Sorry I'm late," said Ms. K. rushing in to the psychotherapy office. "I coach a hockey team."

"You're late?"

"Yeah, by 11 seconds, kiddo."

They sat down in the secluded room. Ms. K. picked up her psychotherapist notepad and flipped through the pages. "Seems that we've covered just about all topics, and everything here says we're good to go."

"You aren't, um, writing down my secrets, are you?"

Ms. K. smiled and flipped out the notepad pages so Joshi could see them. Drawings were the only ink—I'm Not Krazy—on any of the lined pages, and they were very well-crafted pictures. Some were realistic renditions of Joshi's face or of Ms. K.'s moped, and others were cartoons of all sorts. "I've been listening, but I haven't been writing."

"Shinobi Master, am I strong?"

"In some ways, yes."

"Am I strong enough to really protect something?" asked Joshi.

"You are stronger than you know. You are strongest when you protect. Besides, defense and goalkeeping have always been your strong points in hockey."

"But I've never played hockey."

"You should try it sometime, Joshi. And I know you will by your own free will."

"Thanks for the pressure," Joshi sulked.

"No problem, just telling you who you want to be. 'Joshi,' that's just a nickname to go by. Cute, but I don't remember how you ever thought of it."

"I never told you how I thought of it." Joshi reminded her. "My real name is Kiku Nissan. And it also happens to be your name. We—"

"Are the same person, I know. It was my secret, and I told it to someone . . . but I guess it's safe, because that person doesn't exist." Miss K. laughed. "Keen mind. How'd you figure it out?"

Joshi laughed. "Something similar happened in the *Hitherforme* book I'm reading."

"Always did like that novel."

Zippy was in Joshi's room when she came home. Zippy was reading Joshi's journal like it was a tabloid at the grocery store.

"What do you think you're doing?!?"

"Great story, but not romantic, sympathetic, or girly."

"So, that's my life you're talking about," said Joshi.

"You could turn your diary into a *shojo* story, you know, one of those tickle-me-pink magical school life stories."

"I'd rather not, and it's a journal, not a diary." Joshi corrected her.

Zippy waved her hand in the air as if she was shooing away Joshi's words. "First things first. What'll your magical-fighting-girl alibi be?"

"Tomboy Ninja is my alias, and I'm not a magical sissy. I'm just myself."

"CUT! This scene must be fixed. Your name needs something smiley and whimsical in it, happy but brute. How 'bout 'Cherry Razor' or 'Sword Sparkle'? 'Gum-drop madness'? 'Petal Fury?'"

"Those sound like ice cream flavors or perfumes." Joshi remained stoic.

"Okay, fine, Tomboy Ninja, show your weapon."

"My hockey stick, of course."

"CUT! It has to be something pretty and magical, like a staff or baton." The more ridiculous Zippy's ideas were, the more Zippy's 'story' sounded like one Zippy wanted to live herself.

Joshi swung the hockey stick above Zippy's head. "I'm not trading this for anything more harmless."

"Fine, fine, Tomboy Ninja fights with a hockey stick. What's your motto? It should be something about love, friendship, or beauty."

"I know!" Joshi let out a devious laugh. "It shall be 'Destroy All Pink!'"

Whatever it was that Zippy wrote down for a motto, that line was certainly not it. "CUT! You need a better costume. Something cute, flowing, and lots of bows and bells."

"I prefer my cargo pants and b-ball tee just fine."

"CUT! The last thing is, you must be in love."

"You mean, like this?" Joshi drooled at pictures of mopeds in a catalogue.

"You're a failure at this, Joshi. You look more like a videogame hero than a magical girl." ⋆sigh⋆ "I tried to make your life a *shojo*, and instead it's full-blown disaster. Guess you'll always be a ninja."

"Yep, all the way!"

All the world is a comic book and all the people merely characters
I J Y I J Y I J Y
o o o o o o o o o
s s s s s s s s s
h h h h h h h h h
i i i i i i i i i

CHAPTER 19

The chapter that never happened and never will

"Zippy, can I ask you a very important question?" Joshi tried to say in an innocent manner Zippy would appreciate.

"Too late. You already did."

Joshi dropped her fake courtesy and frowned. "What exactly is kringle?"

"You never knew what kringle was? Hmm, how can I describe the savory taste?" Zippy stroked her chin like a wise old man stroking his beard. "Here's a dictionary. Look it up."

"Hej, Zippy, this is a Danish to Japanese dictionary!"

Even Zippy knew more Danish words than kringle. "Du læser gerne, jo?"

Joshi understood what Zippy said, but still didn't know what the one word 'kringle' was. "If you had a different last name, Zippy, it would be Nnoys, Zippy A. Nnoys."

"That I do like! It has a nice ring to it. Then I could say 'This is my friend, Joshi Zingle, and I am Zippy A. Nnoys. Joshi likes kringle and I like boys.'"

"Sorry I mentioned it. I would rather not bother with that topic of yours."

They heard a chorus of dogs barking. The doorbell was ringing.

"No thank you, we're not interested in buying a subscription to *Weirdo* magazine, not today." Zippy closed the door in Raski's face and then reopened it. "But if you're looking for dingoes, come in. Haven't seen many around lately, actually, never seen any at all. How are you, Mr. Fuzzyhead?"

"For once once, I am not here here here here to see you and talk about about about lederhosen, but to to to see Joshi."

Joshi's eyebrowl twitched.

"I I have something something something something something something to give you." A wire extended from Raski's ear and Joshi plugged it into her own. He transmitted a gene in through the wire and into Joshi's brain. "I have given you a copy of my memory-keeping power. From from from from this point on on on on on, you will have clearer memories memories of everything you experience, happy or sad sad. So choose choose your memories wisely wisely wisely wisely."

"Why do this?" Joshi was dumbfounded. "It's great, but why?"

"Someone someone someone suggested I do so so so."

A new chance to make up for the lost memories of Pokey, as Joshi saw it. Speaking of seeing, Joshi suddenly saw nothing, or as it should be said, nothingness in the state of black covering her vision. She couldn't see herself, but she saw someone else. Jÿger came walking towards her, out of the black.

"Hej, Jÿger." The blackness broke away and Joshi saw that she was standing in the middle of reality. Jÿger wore sunglasses. "Jÿger? That's you, isn't it, Jÿger?" With no response from him yet, Joshi poked his shoulder. Or, she meant to poke him. Instead she statically shocked him, waking him up.

"Who is it?"

"Joshi. You know me, don't you?"

Jÿger smiled. "Of's course. I feels sorts of like I justs met someone in reals life that I've knowns through the internet, onlys your exactly the's same. Sorrys I'm driftings off."

"Can you see me?"

"Whens I'm in the World of Nevers I's can. I cames as a refugee intos that world of's yours, inside yours head. I didn'ts wants to disturb you . . . I just thoughts you mights accept me there, away from my's world which sees nothings. I used to sits on the tire swing of the's playground ands hear the others as they rans by. They would wants to taunt me bys spinning the tireswing, buts the onlys thing that saved me's from harm was whens they'd leaves me to go see the unusuals kid, the girl thats would swing all alones and be smelly. They would go ups to her and mocks her in the swings nearby, and she would nevers speak still. I never knews for sure if this girl existeds because I never heards her, she even walked silentlys, like a ninja, untraceables. Until one days I came to hers world, and learned she was a real person."

"It's okay. I accept you in reality like I would aanywhere else . . . hej, Jÿger?" Jÿger seemed busy staring into space again. Joshi left him to enjoy his invisible peace.

"Bye, Joshi." Jÿger waved goodbye. Joshi was in the World of Nevers again. And who did she happen to run into but . . . Zippy, leaning against the arcade wall, as expressionless as Joshi.

"Have you ever gotten a fortune cookie and been so excited to read your fortune, only to see when you take out the piece of paper that it's totally blank on both sides?"

Joshi was certain Zippy was speaking metaphorically until Zippy held up a pile of crumbles with a blank paper sticking out of it.

"What could this mean, Joshi?"

"It's the truth—I mean, a fortune doesn't determine fate. It's all a mystery. You get to write your own fortune, and it will be like no other, like no other life."

"If I could have a life." Whispered Zippy.

"What do you mean? You're definitely more sociable than I am."

"If I literally had a life," said Zippy, "I'm not alive, and I'm not dead like a ghost, either. I'm like a virus, something moving within a body capsule, but having no life, no birth and no death. But I'm not immortal, because a life without death is immortality and I have no life. I'm just a character, a Zippedity Zhong."

"You are lucky to be who you are. Like anyone else, you decided who you wanted to be. If I decided everything about you when I painted the picture of you I wouldn't have made you obsessed with toilets," Joshi joked. "You don't have to put up with real people and real duties and real stress. Like a game, any event or conversation or work you get tired of, you can just quit. You don't even have to learn things, you just magically download the info from people like me and Pokey—well that would also be me. I don't even know half of what Pokey did because her knowledge left with her."

"I've always been jealous of you and your life, so please, promise me you'll make the very most of it!" Zippy sobbed violet-colored tears that matched her eyes.

"I will, Zippy, for you, and me, and everyone else in the world."

How can I just let this world disappear? Would it be selfish to let go of them? Where would the characters go? Joshi wondered.

"Did you just call me 'Shinobi Master'?" asked the psychotherapist sitting in front of Joshi.

"Sorry, I'm not used to Miss K. being gone. She's the only psychotherapist I'd spoken to before you."

Miss Y. slanted her glasses and smiled with pinkish cheeks that matched the pink bow on her suit.

"I've realized something," said Joshi. "When I repaired the paintbrush I found in the trash can by the elevator at the magazine office in Tokyo, I restored part of me that had also been broken. I believed in something that taught me to believe in myself."

"Imagination has a way of repairing reality," said Miss Y. "Sooner than eventually you'll discover that again."

That night in reality Joshi took her medication for the first time in a long time. Strangely enough, she found it on the floor of the bathroom, near the toilet. Ms. Y. had convinced her that the prescribed remedy would calm her inner storm and make her more open to decision-making. "Go where you are needed," was her advice. Joshi felt like she'd just fought a battle. And won.

Chapter 20

Zippy's back!!!

To find out the difference between doom and fate, one must hold up a plaster skull and speak poetically. Talk about the woes of life and how you are so bored with yourself that you are talking to something that does not exist and never will. That is doom. Now, toss aside the skull and sprinkle dirt and water around it so you can anticipate the banzai plant that will grow from it. When moss, not a banzai plant, grows on your skull (not the one connected to your body, but the one made of plaster—hopefully there is a difference), stand back and take a good look at it. It's not what you expected, but nothing is entirely useless. So, you think the moss resembles hair and that makes it look like your favorite president. Because you acted, nature acted, and because you wanted a banzai plant, nature gave you a bunch of moss.

In very much the same way, an author uses fate and doom to their advantage, and for writing endlessly about their own problems disguised in abstract language, they endure catharsis. But if a novel is all about doom, nothing can change fast enough for a decent reaction from either the characters or the reader, and if this author, yours truly, doesn't change topic fast enough, this author realizes they might lose a reader.

This last chapter was doomed but it is also fated to happen, because it is happening now, at the same time as later.

"I've named hims Orange Fungus." said Jÿger, stroking the rabbit he held in his hands but did not see. "He's verys curious abouts you, and that peanut butters smell ons your hands."

Joshi laughed. "He feels exactly like . . ."

". . . the green Orange Fungus. He was the onlys bunny at the pet shop thats had fur with this texture. It's was actually Raski's idea to's get a pets. Raski and Imp are's my owns made up characters, verys much like Zippy is to you. I put part of my memory in Raski."

"If the World of Nevers was taken away, would you never be able to see in any place again?" asked Joshi.

"Understanding you has opened my eyes more than anything."

Joshi fell down. Her heart was strained with an invisible bullet, and her head ached with dizziness. Was it Zippedity?

Or Ioshi? Or both? Which one should it be? Should it be Johan? She wasn't making sense to anyone in her head, not even her conscienceness.

Whatwillyouchoose? Joshi heard. *Whatwillyouchoose?* Slowly it turned into *What-will-you-choose-?* "It's none of your beeswax," said Joshi, wiping earwax from her ears.

"Choose blue!" she heard Lukkar's voice. Looking around her, she did not see Lukkar, but she did pay attention to colors more.

"Yellow is good." Her hair was yellow, and it was rare that she had ever thought about yellow. "Green is good." Leaves were green. She liked leaves, but never saw the green of the leaves as brightly as she did then. "Orange is good." Orange was in the mushroom, the one she'd walked by everyday and had seen as a mushroom, but never before an orange mushroom. "Red is good." Every blue moon, a sunset was red. "Purple is good." Purple was a soft violet, like Zippy's eyes, the shade of foggy clouds at night. "Corndog is good." Corndog was like—

"Hej! So far as I know, 'corndog' isn't a color!"

⋆Burp⋆ Maybe there was more to life than blue. The blue grass, blue sky, blue trees, blue snails, blue me, blue you.

"Pink is stinky."

"Yes, I still hold the opinion that pink is very distasteful." Any color that was not pink was worthy of being blue.

What was Joshi going to do now? Now "To do nothing is to do no evil nor any good. To do something good is to risk doing evil. To have faith is to know no matter what you do, you will get through it. I don't need to do anything or nothing. I don't need reality or the World of Nevers. I just need faith."

The doorbell rang. It did not sound like dogs barking. It sounded like two ⋆dings.⋆ Joshi went to the entryway door cautiously. She opened the door and found a small package outside. She saw Jÿger walking away with other packages under his arm to deliver. The label on her package was marked for "Kiku Nissan". She opened it, and to her horror, found a cell phone. Joshi didn't like phones. Phones made lots of irritable noise, and whenever she answered a phone call, it was never for her.

Joshi looked both ways before she dashed back inside and dropped the cell phone on to her pillow, as if it might vibrate out of control at any given moment or ring until she was deaf. Who could have done this?!?!?!!! She looked at the box it came in, but there was no return address.

After a few silent minutes of careful observation, she clicked it on. The screen flickered, and Joshi plugged her ears and closed her eyes, as if a ladybug would appear on screen. Instead music played in a soft melody that reminded her of a wind-up toy. The cell phone was blue, after all.

Joshi set down the telephone. What was she thinking? She wanted to leave immediately, to run and hide . . . It was time to re-discover reality as it was, if that made any sense. She started packing a few items in her bag. She would back in a few hours, by nightfall and by then she would have dreamed another lifetime in her memories, if not for reality.

Music played, the sound of Joshi's favorite song, one Lise played every morning on the piano. How long had it been since she'd heard it? It had been years since this morning, Joshi felt. After the song played twice the phone made a beep and Zippy's voice came on: "Hello, you're supposed to answer the phone!"

Joshi not only picked up the phone, but she also surprised herself when she held it up to her right ear. "Hello."

"What's up?"

Why do some people constantly need to be reminded what up is? "Up is the opposite of down, Zippy."

"So, why are you packing up stuff? Ready to go somewhere?"

"Yeah, I'm going to explore all of reality, to see the whole world as it really looks li—hey, how do you know what I'm doing?"

"I haven't left your head yet . . . no, actually I'm calling from a pay phone and I'm on my way out into reality as well—"

"But how can you do that? I thought it wasn't possible because you're . . ."

"The way I am now it is not possible, but things are changing, for a price," said Zippy.

"Explain, please."

"This phone of yours has an unlimited battery, and it can never be turned off."

Darn! Joshi wished she had never turned it on.

Zippy kept talking. "When you go off on your own, someone will have to keep track of you. I'm calling to say farewell, because I know you are leaving the World of Nevers, and you'd say goodbye sooner or later. I've gone to the Character Data Center already, and everything's arranged. I just have to give the word, and I'll—"

"No! You can't give up your personality."

"Oh, not that, I'm keeping that. Just think of this as an example of how pets really are like their owners," said Zippy.

That explanation did not make any sense to Joshi. "What will happen?"

"When I qualify as a person, I will meet you in Heaven. Oh, and I am sorry for writing in your diary."

"You're not sorry. And it's a journal, not a diary."

"One more thing: if you write a novel about me, will you mention my uncanny affinity for mugs with lids?"

". . . Is that your new obsession?"

"I really like how the line sounds, like something you would read on the back of a book." Zippy paused, perhaps because her thoughts were racing too fast to articulate. "See you later, Kiku."

"See you later, Zippedity."

Joshi opened her journal and flipped through the pages till she identified Zippy's handwriting. "Dear Diary, I am sorry to inform you that I am retiring from my position as a multicolored alien dog." Weird. "Now that I am moving on to a new future, I will also not be able to fill the role of Joshi's best friend." It was very sentimental to read a heartfelt message, but at the same time Joshi was also relieved that Zippy hadn't snuck a trap inside her journal. Joshi could imagine Zippy's voice as she read the next line. "Joshi is the biggest weirdo I have ever met." For Zippy to say that about her felt like a compliment to Joshi. She was closing the book when the page flipped over and she saw more of Zippy's handwriting.

"As this task is very important, I have successfully trained a replacement to fill the post of 'best friend.'" And if Joshi ever read what an old friend wrote in her diary, ahem, I mean, 'journal,' then she would see Hitoshi's phone number listed at the bottom of the page."

Who did Zippy think she was . . . ? Zippy was being, well . . . Zippy. Joshi closed her journal and put it in her backpack. She shut the latch of her backpack, swung it over her shoulder and turned the doorknob to leave her room when . . .

A song was playing, Joshi's very own theme song, the wonderful, mystical, joshi-cal song of a dusty church organ she had not heard in a very long time. Joshi couldn't help but go closer to the phone on her bed like a moth drawn to a glowing light. She also couldn't help but notice the name "Hitoshi" had come up on the cell phone screen.

At 4:00 pm, July 13, 2005, Zippedity Zhong left inexistence and entered the path of the living. A child with her spirit (and her good looks, if she might say so herself) was born as Yoshi Yang Tokio, and she experienced her very first memory that day. Nine years later, the following report was heard on Joshi's radio about the former inexistent-being:

> *Today in Tokyo, a world record was set by Japan's very own Yoshi Tokio. Ms. Tokio may seem like an ordinary girl, with a pink bow in her hair and a smile on her face, but she has just broken the world record of number of flights of stairs jumped down on a pogo stick by jumping up and down 105 flights of stairs, all in the same day. Now, you kiddos, don't try this at home because Ms. Tokio, or "Y" as she likes to be called, is a professional stunter. Her hobbies also include plumbing, knocking down doors, and studying time travel. However, she doesn't see stunt acting as a lifelong career. She says that when she grows up she would like to be a psychotherapist. Amazing kid, that Yoshi.*

Back in 2005, Joshi answered her ringing cell phone.

"Hello?"

"Hello, Joshi. This is Jÿger." Zippy was probably pulling a prank by programming Hitoshi's name to match Jÿger's number.

"Oh, hi Jÿger."

"I'ms glad you openeds the package. The cell phone thing was my idea. Hope you don't mind communicating this way."

Why couldn't they just be pen pals? Joshi hid her antisocial feelings. "Oh, it's fine. Thank you, and thanks to Zippy too. This cell phone must be expensive to work the way it does." *Okay, just wrap up the conversation so I won't need to talk . . .*

"Have you written any more stories lately?" Joshi's first fan! This was cool.

"Uh, no . . . but I have been painting." Wait, why'd she say that? What good could that do for Jÿger?

"Tell me about your art!"

"Well, my latest piece is of a wolf I saw when I was at the zoo yesterday. It's been named Runaroundandpaint'em, ironically. It was gray and fuzzy with extra whisps of fur sticking out of its heels. In the painting, I used extra paint in a curved stroke on the fur so it would have more texture. The eyes are triangles with rounded corners . . ." and Joshi went on with every detail.

"I like the way you talk about your art. You make each picture complicated, but deep and recognizable to the soul, like an emotion." Was it her, or had Jÿger started talking differently?

"Thanks, Jÿger. You really are my only fan."

"Now that we're both in reality, I want you to call me by my real name. Jÿger is my middle name. My first name is Hitoshi." So, Hitoshi hadn't disappeared off the face of the earth. Interesting.

"I'm really Kiku, in reality, Kiku Nissan, but I'm still Joshi. Actually, I'm going to call myself Jaaski now. It's not a given name, but it's the next stage after being Joshi."

"I think that's kewl. 'Jaaski' is pronounced the same way as 'Joshi' and 'Yoshi,' so you're the same as before, only different."

Jaaski never ceased to be amazed by her friends' odd ability to discern the spelling of words spoken in purely verbal conversations.

Hitoshi continued. "That name suits you well. You never stop creating, and that's a big part of who you are. I think it is a 'given name,' for you gave it to yourself."

"Thanks. I think Hitoshi is a wonderful name for you. You also maintain an identity that is what you want it to be."

"Hitoshi, do you know what happened to Imp, Snarg, Qrsis, and the rest of them? Did they just disintegrate?" asked Jaaski.

"No," said Hitoshi. "Don't be sad about closing up that place. It's like the fate of this world, a new universe was created, one that is the only universe in existence, the one where the spirits of our friends were released into the minds of others needing comfort. It's how I found my guardian angel. Continue to travel the world, and you shall meet up with people that remind you of them and have the odd dream-like memories of your characters."

"We could find all of them, all but Zippy, who is her own person now. She has her own spirit, but she gave up her memory to do it," said Jaaski.

"It is good for her that she could to start a life that would not be burdened by any past guilt. You will always have memories of her, remember?" A very Hitoshi-ish pun.

"Yes, enough memories to share when I find her; and if I cannot, I shall search the past, my past, and Pokey's."

"Will you call me some time, Jaaski?"

Jaaski smiled really big. "Yes, Hitoshi, I promise."

Jaaski's train reached the first railroad station of her first destination. "Denmark," she whispered, "is full of the past." Her lightweight backpack held all she needed: her cell phone, a sketchbook with paints and paintbrush, some slices of kringle, and a train ticket.

"Sorry." Some English-speaker had just stepped on her heel behind her. She turned her head and faced the girl.

"Hej, Lise."

Lise? Here?

Lise held a suitcase with a "Just been to Reykjavik" bumper sticker on it. In her other hand she grasped the handle to a wheeled a telescope case. "Hej, Jaaski. What are you doing here?"

"Searching the past."

"Well, I've been all over the world looking for you, and I've looked one place you'd never guess—the future."

"So the past rests in Denmark and the future rests in Iceland. Where's the present? Could it be . . . Japan?"

"Jaaski," Lise smirked, "What are we going to do with you?"

"I think the question is 'What am I going to do with myself?'" Jaaski scratched her head.

"It would make a good book, all you've experienced," said Lise. "You could jot it all down and get a career writing abstract fiction, as it is called in the future."

"Fighting abstract fiction?"

"I said *writing*."

"Oh. Yeah, really. My autobiography as award-winning fiction."

Lise leaned in closer and whispered in Jaaski's ear. "For all the world is a comic book, and all the people merely characters."

Till we meet again!

About the Author

Rune Marie Nielsen is a comic artist, painter, and writer who enjoys playing video games, learning foreign languages, and traveling abroad. Her first comic was published at age twelve and she has since written fiction and nonfiction for various magazines and journals. Her favorite foods are cheesecake and sardines, though she advises that the two do not produce good results when mixed together.